HARTL HOUSE: HOMECOMING

-Book 2-

The Hartley House Hauntings

EVE S EVANS

ALSO BY

EVE S EVANS

Fiction:

The Haunting of Hartley House
Hartley House Homecoming
The Haunting of Crow House
The Haunting of Redburn Manor

Anthologies:

True Ghost Stories of First Responders
50 Terrifying Ghost Stories
Real Ghost Stories
Shadow People
Chilling Ghost Stories
Haunted Hotels
Haunted Hospitals
Haunted Objects
Haunted People
Haunted Suburbs
Voices From Beyond

This book is dedicated to an amazing person I met along my journey into the paranormal. You truly have become someone special in my life.

Follow Eve and her books on Goodreads or Bookbub! And get notified of any new reads coming in 2021.

The following story is fictional. Any resemblance to real persons, places, things, or events is merely coincidental.

All rights reserved. No part of this publication may be transmitted or reproduced in any form or by any means. This includes photocopying, electronic, mechanical, or by storage system (informational or otherwise), unless given written permission by the author.
Copyright © May 2021 Eve S. Evans
Cover By: Penny Dreadful

prologue

The candles guttered around the circle, dancing faintly in an invisible draught sweeping in from somewhere further in the house.

Nadia watched them closely, worried they would go out completely and strand them all in darkness.

Joe had his eyes closed, his head swaying faintly side to side, his fists curled against the table. He'd told the group that he'd made contact with the presence of a child, who was watching them from the corner of the room. When Nadia glanced over there, trying to pick through the shadows, she saw nothing. A chill crawled along her arms, and she felt the unnerving sensation of being watched by invisible eyes.

She returned her attention to Joe. His eyes were fluttering beneath his lids, almost like he was dreaming.

His breathing hitched suddenly, and his eyes flew open. They seemed almost to bulge from his head, stretching the skin around them, wider than they ought to be. Nadia's chest clenched, and for a moment, a shadow passed over his face, as though the candles had gone out only for Joe.

Amie leaned forward in her seat, her face ghastly in the candlelight. "Joe, what is it? Is something wrong?"

Opposite Nadia, Max and Sam exchange an uneasy glance. The tension around the table had increased twofold, and Nadia's heart quickened in response. She reached up and tucked a strand of hair that had escaped her ponytail behind her ears. She didn't like having her vision obscured, not being able to see if anything was creeping towards her from her periphery.

She flicked another glance to the corner. For a moment, the shadows there seemed thicker. Something moved among them.

Next to her, Trish stared closely at Joe, her eyes narrowed and her lips slack. She looked uncertain, fear etched across her face. Was something wrong? She didn't understand what was happening.

In the corner of the room, something moved in the dark. Nadia thought she heard a faint growl, almost animalistic in nature. Fear clenched her throat. Joe cried out suddenly, his face twisting. "No... you're not..."

Nadia's eyes tracked the movement in the darkness, watching a shadow bleed away from the coagulating gloom and move across the room towards them. Her fingers clenched against the table, and she fought against her instinct to run.

"Joe-"

"No, stay away," he cried, his whole body seizing up. "You're the one causing this... you're..."

Amie and Max stared across at Joe with unabashed horror. Nadia felt fear curl in her gut.

"Joe, what is it?" Amie asked urgently.

"It's not... you must leave. You don't belong here," Joe said, his voice becoming low and tortured, his features twisting as though in pain.

Nadia felt something brush past her, heard that same low, guttural murmur. "It's here. It's in here with us," she whispered, her voice pinched. "I saw something."

"Joe, come back to us," Amie urged, but the medium either wasn't listening, or he couldn't hear.

He threw back his head, letting out a low cry. "No, get away."

"We need to bring him back," Max said. "Joe, can you hear me? Break away from it. Come back to us."

His Adam's apple bobbed visibly against his throat, a bead of sweat rolling down the side of his head.

"Joe?"

His head snapped forward suddenly, and he slumped over, panting heavily.

When Nadia glanced at him, something about his face seemed off. Unfamiliar. His pupils were dilated, almost filling the whites of his eyes with darkness, and his skin seemed particularly ashen, as though all the blood had been drained from his face.

Then he blinked, and his pupils contracted, and he looked like Joe again. He cleared his throat gently, still breathing hard. "Well, I think that means we should end the session."

The others stared at him. "Joe, what happened?" Amie asked, but Joe ignored her.

"I'm now closing the session," he said to the room. "Spirits can no longer reach out to me."

Then he reached forward, and blew the candles out, one by one.

"What the hell, Joe!" Trish exclaimed as the room around them plunged into absolute darkness.

Something uneasy swirled inside Nadia. She didn't like this, didn't like the way Joe was acting. What had happened to the spirit he was speaking with? What had caused the sudden change in his demeanor? It had almost seemed like he'd been possessed, yet he'd blinked it away so quickly.

"You could have at least let us get the lights first," Sam muttered irritably. There was the sound of someone scraping back their chair, and then the sound of footsteps scurrying towards the table from the corner of the room. "What the hell?" Sam said, just as a low growl cut across the room, deep and guttural.

"Guys-" Trish started, just as Sam yelped, a flurry of movement in the dark. Something sharp and jagged cut through her trousers, slicing the skin on her leg. Warm blood immediately began to pool from the cut, and she fell back onto her chair with a pained grunt.

"Sam? What the hell is happening?" Max said from beside her, his voice strained and panicked in the dark.

Nadia felt herself begin to tremble. Something unseen was attacking them in the dark. "Someone get the lights! Quickly!"

"I'm on it," Joe gasped, scraping his chair back and hurrying towards the switch on the wall. A second later, there was a thud and the sound of something cracking – bones or wood or something else.

"Joe? Joe, are you okay?" Amie said, her voice tight with panic.

Nobody responded, and everything had gone eerily quiet. Only Sam's stifled cries of pain and the heavy panting of everyone in the room.

"Joe?"

Nothing.

Without a word, everyone around the table rose to their feet and began inching forward through the darkness, hands outstretched to the wall.

Nadia's heart thudded painfully in her chest, each breath ripping down her throat. What the hell was happening? Where was Joe?

Her foot hit something on the ground, and she jerked forward, landing heavily on her knees with a dull crack. The thing on the floor was strangely soft and malleable, and something cracked beneath her foot when she hit it.

A body.

Joe felt sick. His head spun and his heart pounded with dread, each thud threatening to burst straight through his chest.

Bile tore up his throat, burning the back of his mouth, but he swallowed it back, fumbling with blood-slicked fingers as he tried to dial the numbers on his cell phone. He cursed softly, blood gleaming thickly on the screen as he held it against his ear, praying for the call to connect.

There was a delay, the soft crackle of static, and then finally-

"911, what's your emergency?"

He swallowed back the taste of bile and blood, almost choking on his words. "I think someone is dead. Please... hurry."

Chapter ONE

Nadia cupped her face with a sigh, staring at the blank screen in front of her.

A new deadline was coming up in a few days, and her laptop chose to break now. It had been fine the last time she'd checked, but now the screen was completely black and nothing would turn on, no matter how many buttons she pressed. Did it have some kind of computer virus? Or was it just on its way out? It was getting pretty old after all; she'd written most of her bestselling novels on this trusty old thing. Maybe it was about time for a change.

Blowing out a sigh, she slammed the lid of the laptop closed and scraped back her chair, stretching out of it. She'd not slept well last night, and her body felt strangely lethargic, not quite moving as fast as it normally would. More strange, haunting dreams. The same ones she hadn't been able to shake since childhood.

She trudged out of her office and went downstairs to retrieve the morning paper. It was on her front step as it always was, but the paper was more crinkled than usual and it was covered in a fine layer of dirt, as though it had been left out a while.

"Tch," she muttered, brushing off the dirt and straightening out the crinkles as she took it into the kitchen, setting it down on the table. Reading the paper would have to suffice until the local repair shop opened and she could take her laptop to get fixed. If it was still fixable.

Perusing through the pages, the main headline that caught her attention was something about the commercial fishing market becoming crowded recently. Some kind of crisis with whales and dolphins and other things she had only limited interest in.

As she was about to turn the page, a heavy knock against her front door interrupted her. She flicked a glance to the kitchen clock; it was still relatively early, and she wasn't expecting anyone to visit today.

Folding closed the newspaper, she pushed herself to her feet and paused, her gaze hovering over the front page. She hadn't noticed before, but the date on the paper was wrong. It was two weeks old. It would explain the gritty state of it, but why would a two-week old paper be lying on her step? Must have been a mistake, she supposed. Or the neighbors were stealing her papers now.

Another knock rattled against the front door, and she flinched, quickly turning away from the table.

"I'm coming, I'm coming," she muttered, unlatching the door and opening it.

Amie was standing on the front porch, her blond hair in disarray and her cheeks clammy despite the early sun.

"Amie, what-"

"Did you see the news?" The woman interrupted, pushing past Nadia and walking straight in, her boots tracking dirt onto the tiles.

Nadia gave a start, but quickly shut the door behind her and turned to follow Amie into the kitchen. "Only something about dolphins and a commercial fishing crisis," she said with a loose shrug. "Why? What's up?"

"Hartley is what's up," Amie said distractedly. "Where's your laptop?"

"Upstairs," Nadia said, and Amie immediately started for the stairs. "But wait, it's busted. Won't turn on. Just tell me."

Amie turned to face her, wringing her hands together. "Hartley House sold again," she said breathlessly, her cheeks appearing gaunt as she sucked in a breath. "Everyone was murdered in the basement."

For a moment, Nadia felt faint, and she reached out to catch herself against the wall. "What?" She whimpered, pulling herself over to the kitchen table and collapsing in one of the chairs. Her legs were shaking. "What do you mean?"

"Exactly what it sounds like. Hartley House has killed again."

"But... but how? I thought we stopped it. Didn't we cleanse it?"

Amie dropped her eyes, a frown shadowing her face. "That's the thing..." she said solemnly. "Can I... ask you something? It might sound a little odd, but hear me out okay?"

Nadia nodded, and Amie slipped into the seat opposite her. She raked a hand through her hair, which seemed more greasy and unkempt than usual, hanging over her face in thin strands. She looked just as tired as Nadia felt; she had the same dark circles around her eyes. "How much of the last day do you actually remember?"

Nadia stared at her, swallowing. "Well... I remember falling... no, being *pushed* down the stairs. That hurt like hell, and I ended up staying in bed for the rest of the evening." She paused, lowering her eyes to the table as she tried to recollect the rest of the memory. Every time she reached for it, it fell away like sand through her fingers, too many pieces to put back together. "But... honestly, that's it. I can't remember what else happened. I guess I must have been pretty tired. Why?"

Amie leaned forward on her elbows, forcing Nadia to meet her gaze. "Because it's not just you. I don't remember either."

"What?" Nadia blurted, her heart thudding quickly in her chest. "What do you mean?"

"That last day at Harley House... I have no memory of it either."

"But... but didn't we cleanse it?" Nadia said. "Didn't we cleanse all of the negative energy, exorcise the spirits?"

Nadia saw Amie gulp, shaking her head. "I've spoken to the entire team about it," she said. "But nobody can remember what happened on that last day either."

"I... I don't understand. What does it mean?"

Amie leaned back in her chair, looking at Nadia beneath a shadowed gaze. "It means we have to go back. Hartley House is still haunted, and this time, we have to finish the job."

Chapter TWO

Nadia never thought she would be back so soon. To the house that stole her parents and changed the rest of her life.

It looked almost exactly the same as the last time she was here, tall and brooding, wreathed in gloom. The grimy brown bricks were the same, and the crumbling tiles. But the ivy had been trimmed since the last time – presumably by the newest owners – and the windows were not as vacant as she remembered, covered with cream-colored curtains that moved gently in an interior draught.

But despite its new appearance, it still *felt* the same. Burgeoning with something dark and unnatural, something that didn't belong.

On the front lawn, amidst the tangle of brown grass and long, jagged weeds, a sign reading SOLD swung back and forth in the wind on creaking hinges. It should never had been put up for market. Another family.

Another tragedy. They thought they'd stopped all of this. They thought they'd stopped all the death and bloodshed that would happen here. So why was another family dead? Why had more blood been spilled?

Amie and Nadia stared solemnly at the house, neither willing to make a move. Despite her hatred for the place, even after all this time, she could still feel it calling to her. It still wouldn't let her go. That's why she was back here, standing before it once again. Because she couldn't let it go either.

"You ready?" Amie said, glancing across at her.

Nadia didn't return the gaze. "No," she muttered honestly. "I don't think I'll ever be ready. Not to go through everything again." She sucked in a deep breath, expelling it slowly. "But I'm here now. So, let's go."

Amie nodded, her blond hair stirring in the wind, and walked up the front door. It had been given a fresh coat of paint, and the old metal knocker had been removed, but Nadia could still see the shadow of the old door beneath – the dark, peeling wood and the grimy stains. It was always there, no matter how much you painted over it or covered it, the old Hartley was still underneath, waiting to surface again.

Amie slid the key into the lock, and the tumblers inside clicked into place.

Nadia's chest tightened, and she fought against the urge to flee. It would do no good in the end. No matter how far she ran, Hartley would always call her back.

A car door slammed from behind them, and the rest of the team – Sam, Max, Trish and Joe – came up the driveway in silence.

"We're all here?" Amie asked nobody in particular, twisting the handle and letting the shadows seep out. "Then let's get inside."

The inside was not the same as she remembered. The house had been cleaned up, new flooring laid down, each room re-decorated and furnished. Everything seemed strangely new and artificial. Covering up the dirt and blood that stained the house underneath it all.

Nadia walked through the hallway, swallowing back the flutter of anxiety she felt. Why was she back here? After all this time, the house still couldn't let her go. Or was it the other way round? Could she not let go of the house? She found herself drawn back here despite all of the warnings in her head, all of the dreams telling her to stay away.

The others came in behind her, carrying their equipment behind them. They were more solemn than usual, not the talkative bunch of investigators they had been before.

"We'll get set up," Amie said, "and then have a meeting to discuss what we're going to do. Sound good?"

The others nodded, filing into the front room, but Nadia stayed where she was, staring at the interior of the house. It had all changed, and yet it was still the same. Nadia could feel it in her bones that it was still the same house. The energy they should have cleansed was still here, just as strong as before.

The memories, the lingering echoes of that night, were all still here, waiting for her to come back…

The house was thick with gloom. Nadia didn't remember it ever being this dark before. There was always a light on somewhere, threading through the house with a warm, inviting glow. It wasn't late enough for her parents to have gone to bed either, which is why it felt so odd. The whole hallway was shattered into fragments of darkness, some places darker than the rest, making it seem like it was moving.

She felt blindly along the wall, trying to find the switch for the lamp. When she found it, the bulb stuttered faintly to life, but immediately dimmed again, barely casting enough light to illuminate the end of the hallway.

Nadia swallowed, a chill moving along her bare arms.

Why was it so cold, so dark, so silent? Where were her parents?

It almost felt like the house was empty, like her parents weren't home. But they couldn't have left; the front door was unlocked, and her dad's car was still in the drive. They had *to be here.*

"Mom? Dad?" She called quietly, unwilling to disturb the silence with her voice. "I came home early."

She heard no movement beyond the silence. Heard no voices respond to her call.

Tiptoeing forward, her slippers shuffling against the floorboards, she moved towards the living room. She couldn't hear the television playing, couldn't see any lights flashing from beneath the doorway.

Hesitating outside the door, she rested her fingers against the wood.

The smell struck her first. A wave of heavy, putrefied air washed out, making her stomach twist with nausea.

What was that smell?

Part of her was terrified of stepping inside. Somehow, she knew something had happened. Something horrible waited for her on the other side.

Dread flooded her body, and she stepped forward tentatively.

"Mom?" She whispered, her voice tight with fear. "Dad? Please, answer me."

The darkness inside was complete, creeping along her vision. The hallway lamp flickered, dimming even further.

As her eyes adjusted, she saw something on the floor in the middle of the room. A figure, stretched out by the kitchen door.

"M-Mom?" She cried, rushing forward, paying no attention to the darkness swirling around her. "Mom, no."

Her slippers skidded over something wet on the floor, and the smell hit her all at once. Blood.

It was everywhere. All over the floor, on her mother's body, smeared over her face and in her hair. Her eyes were wide open, shrouded with death.

Mom… Dad… Why did you have to die? Why did you have to leave me all alone…

"Why," she whispered to nobody in particular, letting her voice linger on the silence. "I guess I couldn't keep away after all. I'm tied here, just like these ghosts."

She swallowed back her voice, reaching out to press her hand against the wall, soaking up the memories that she had here.

Back before the murder, before all the blood and death, when she'd had a happy childhood, loving parents. She tried to remember the good memories. But she couldn't. It was all overshadowed now, stained by the tragedy that had happened eleven years ago. There were no good memories here. There never had been. The house had stolen them all away when it had stolen her parents. When she had learned of the house's terrible history, awash in murder and suicide. There were no happy recollections here, for her or anyone who stayed here.

Amie poked her head out of the doorway ahead of her, making Nadia jump. "You coming?" She asked, arching her brows.

Nadia swallowed, shaking away the remembrances that had settled on her like dust. "Yeah. I'll be right there."

Chapter THREE

Nadia shuffled her legs for the fifth time, feeling the cushions dip beneath her. She felt oddly uncomfortable in the new surroundings. The plush cream sofa she was sitting on felt out of place in the house, like it didn't belong; it was too new, too bright and clean for a house that still felt so dirty and dark. She could still feel the years of dust that lingered here, settling on her skin like an itch.

Amie and the others were setting up their equipment around the rest of the house, cameras and audio and motion sensors, just like last time.

Joe was in the kitchen. Nadia could see him through the doorway, pacing across the room and muttering to himself under his breath with his fists clenched either side of him.

Pushing herself off the sofa, she moved over to the kitchen doorway and leaned against it, crossing her arms over her chest.

"You okay, Joe?" she said gently.

He looked up, startled, before quickly recovering himself. "The energy in the house," he said, shaking his head vigorously. "It's just as strong as it was before. I don't understand why. I thought we cleansed the place, last time we were here."

Nadia nodded, looking down at her feet. "Yeah, I don't really get it either. Don't you think it's strange that none of us remember doing it though?"

Joe stopped pacing, coming to stand opposite her. "You don't remember either?"

Nadia shook her head, pursing her lips before eventually speaking: "I feel terrible about it. Like it's my fault this family got killed. I thought the house was safe again, I let another family move in here. And now look what happened. They're all dead. All because of the house. Because of me."

Joe stayed quiet, basking in his own thoughts. Then he hesitantly reached out and touched Nadia's arm. A faint tingle went through her. "Don't blame yourself," he said softly. "If anything, it's all of our fault. We came here to cleanse the house, and yet somehow it didn't work." He shrugged. "We're here to make things right again, okay?"

Nadia nodded and Joe let his arm fall back to his side, shifting his glance over Nadia's shoulder.

"You got everything set up?" He asked, and Nadia glanced back to see Max coming into the room, fiddling with some equipment in his hand.

He glanced up, his eyes moving between them both. "Just about," he said. "Audio and visual equipment's done. Amie and the others are just setting up motion detectors in the hallway. You two alright down here?"

Nadia glanced at Joe, but he had plastered a smile on his face. "Yep, all good here," he said, and Nadia thought it odd he didn't mention about the energy when he had seemed so troubled by it before.

"Great. Well, the others should be here soon and then we can get started. Although knowing Amie, she'll probably insist on getting lunch first," he said with a dry chuckle.

Nadia allowed a small smile. She could see the unease still lingering behind Max's smile, but at least he was trying to ease the tensions somewhat.

"Do you think we'll be able to cleanse the house properly this time?" Nadia asked carefully, her mind still lingering on the words Joe had said earlier. *We're here to make things right again...* "How will we know that this time, it worked?"

Joe licked his lips. "I'll be able to feel if there's a shift in energy," he said. "And if we do everything right, it should all fall into place."

"But last time… why didn't it work last time? That's what I don't understand?" Nadia continued. Joe shuffled his feet, like the questions were bothering him.

"I don't either," Max said before Joe could respond. "It's weird. Something just doesn't feel right about this whole thing. But there's no point worrying about it now. Let's just do our jobs and make this house safe again."

Nadia nodded, but part of her was unconvinced that Hartley House could ever be *safe* again, that it could ever be *normal* again. After so many years of death and murder, could a house simply… change? She knew she was subscribing living qualities to nothing but bricks and mortar, but in a way, the House *was* alive, at least in her head. The energy that lingered here gave it that feeling of corporeal existence, like it had a mind of its own. Rather than seeing spirits as individuals, they all congregated here into a single entity, a mass feeling of vengeance and anger among the guilt and regret.

"You okay, Nadia? You look like you've got a lot going on up there," Max said gently, and she glanced up at him, forcing a smile.

"Yeah, just trying to think things through," she said. "Anyway, what-"

The words were drowned out beneath the sound of something heavy thudding against the ceiling above them, hard enough to rattle the light fixture and make the doorway vibrate beneath Nadia's arm.

"What the hell?" Joe muttered as a light shower of dust rained down from the ceiling.

"Must be the others," Max said nonchalantly, brushing a cloud of grey dirt from his shoulder.

"No, that wasn't them," Joe warned, staring hard at the ceiling with a crease between his brows.

Three figures appeared at the living room doorway, and Amie, Sam and Trish came in looking wide-eyed.

"Did you guys hear that?" Trish asked incredulously, shaking her head. "Sounded like something heavy."

"Yeah, what do you think it was?" Sam added, flicking a nervous glance to the ceiling.

Nobody had an answer.

Joe cleared his throat gently. "Well, whatever it was, it wants us to know it's here," he said.

Just as he said that, Nadia glimpsed a shadow out of the corner of her eye, moving across the kitchen. It was fleeting, not lasting long enough for her to track it, but it made her head thump and her knuckles clench.

"Nadia? Are you-"

The rest of Amie's words were lost beneath the screech of metal against the linoleum as one of the chairs tucked beneath the kitchen table slid out on its own, rocketing across the floor and thudding into the cabinet opposite.

Joe visibly flinched, spinning on his heel to see the chair, still shuddering slightly from the impact. He gulped. "Yep. We're definitely not alone."

Chapter FOUR

Joe breathed in the cold, wet air, feeling it move sluggishly against the back of his throat. The others were still inside, doing some preliminary investigation of the house, but Joe needed a break. He was finding it stifling being stuck in the house. Difficult to breathe. Even out here, his throat felt clogged and tight, like he couldn't get enough air into his body.

    He ambled slowly around the property, his hands in his pockets, lifting his eyes up to linger on the brown vines creeping up along the walls, the knee-length weeds and thistles sprouting in the garden. The crumbling stone and missing tiles, neglected and ruined. It was all still the same. He'd never wanted to come back, but he'd had no choice. The house had called him back, like it had called back so many others, trapping them within its labyrinthine walls like a spider traps a fly, wrapping it up in a web of deceit. A trap nobody could escape, no matter how much they tried to break free.

Sweat threaded along his brow, despite the chilly wind. Even outside the house, his thoughts were racing through his mind and he was barely able to keep up with them all. His heart thudded erratically in his chest, and his body felt like it was coiled tight, almost as though he was on the verge of a panic attack.

What had happened here, what he had seen and felt, what he had done… it had all tangled together in one thick, knotted rope, and the longer he stayed here, the tighter he could feel it getting around his neck, squeezing the air from his lungs. Guilt for the past, fear for the future. It was all here, echoing through the house, calling to him. He had to finish what he had started here. He couldn't leave until everything was the way it should be.

He stopped beside a well at the back of the property. The crumbling stone structure was already in the midst of decay, the bricks grimy and trenched with weeds and moss. He reached out and pressed his fingers to the bricks, the brown-green moss spongy and soft, and peered down into the darkness of the well.

The water at the bottom was stagnant and dark, nothing but a glimmering reflection. If he stared hard enough, he might make out the shape of his own face peering back at him, pale and haggard. Not the person he had wanted to be. Not the person he used to know. Someone different. Someone changed by the past.

As he stared into that darkness, letting the smell of silt and damp wash over him, he found himself wondering what life would have been like if none of this had happened, if he hadn't been called back here like this, to finish what he'd started.

He'd been on the road to success. His last television interview had attracted an abundance of attention to his career; people all over the country had wanted a glimpse of his talents, required use of his services. He was one of the upcoming, high profile psychics. One interview had turned into two, three, four. Television hosts invited him onto their shows, he'd been booked for speaking engagements. He'd even landed a book deal to write about his experiences and his life. Everything had seemed to happen at once. His life had become exciting and meaningful again. He left everything else behind, focusing on the promising future ahead of him. All of his hard work, finally paying off, giving him the recognition he deserved. No longer held back by disappointment and failure.

Until Hartley called him back. Until the dreams and the visions and the haunting nightmares that wouldn't go away, wouldn't leave him alone. Not until he dragged himself back here, not until he faced his demons.

He wanted to do it all. He wanted to be famous. He wanted to attend all of those television interviews and speaking engagements, he wanted to sign the book deal and write about his life, so that people knew what he'd been through, knew what he was capable of. He wanted people to know him, to see him and his talent. To be recognized and praised.

But now it all seemed pointless, *futile*. He wouldn't get his happy ending after all. Part of him always knew that since the last time he walked out. He would *always* come back. That was the way these things worked. Once Hartley got a grip on you, they didn't let go. You were a doll for them to play with, to taunt and manipulate.

Lifting his eyes away from the well, Joe let his gaze rise to the trees that bordered the property, huddled close together to form a tight, knotted canopy. He could barely see the rays of sunlight beyond their branches, misting the air with nothing but a faint yellow light. No warmth penetrated the trees. It was cold here, just like inside the house. A permanent chill that resided in the walls and in the floorboards, in the bricks and stones and foundations.

Then the sun dipped back behind a cloud, the world went dark.

Glancing back down at the well, nothing but a vague, shadowy shape stared back, lost to the darkness.

With his body as tight and knotted as the trees, he turned back around to face Hartley House, letting his eyes linger on the fading bricks, the peeling paint, the vacant windows, where eyes watched unseen from the darkness.

The House that wouldn't let go. The House that wasn't finished with him.

Then he lowered his head in surrender and began to walk back, dragging his feet through the grass as the weeds and the thistles latched onto his ankles.

Sometimes, the most amazing things happened just a moment too late.

Chapter FIVE

Nothing but the soft clink of dishes from the kitchen and the crackle of the fire could be heard among the stillness of the afternoon. Nadia and the others were sitting around the fireplace while Trish and Amie finished clearing up from their late lunch.

Max and Sam were hunched over the coffee table, watching the camera display on Max's tablet. Each corner of the screen displayed a visual from each of the cameras they had set up around the house, giving them a clear view of each room. Joe was sitting across from Nadia, staring ruminatively into the fire as he twisted his fingers around in his lap.

Nadia could tell something was bothering him. Everyone had been quiet since the spirits had blatantly taunted them with their presence, almost as though they knew the guilt they were triggering by reminding them of their failure the last time they were here.

Nadia's own head was feeling particularly heavy and crowded with thoughts. Being back here, back in the room where she'd found her mother lying dead in a pool of her own blood, was dredging up memories she thought she had banished deep into her subconscious. Memories she thought she had cleansed when they cleansed the house the last time they were here. But just like the spirits who remained, those memories lingered, just as strong and vivid as the night they had happened. Strong enough that she could almost still smell the blood on the floor, the horrible stench of something rotting in the dark. Her mother's body, still festering somewhere in the shadows of the house, a memory of blood that could never be scrubbed away.

Nadia hummed quietly to herself.

She was sitting on the floor in the living room, playing with a raggedy-looking doll that she had named Avaline. It had been a present from her mother when she was small, and even years later, after time had worn away at the color of her eyes and thinned out the fabric of her dress, she was still one of Nadia's favorite toys.

She ran her fingers gently through its hair, humming a tune her mom usually sang for her before bed. She had a comb for her that she'd lost some time ago, so instead she used her fingers to brush the stray strands of hair back into place.

Nadia froze suddenly as she heard something thud in the hallway, hitting the wall on the other side of the living room. She waited, her fingers still resting on Avaline's head as she listened hard to whatever it was.

A second later, she heard her mother's hurried footsteps coming down the hall. She knew it was her mother because of the shuffling pad of the slippers she wore indoors.

"Are you okay?" She heard her mom asked, her voice muffled through the wall. Who was she speaking to? Nadia's father?

After a quiet grunt, she heard her father respond in a short, harsh voice. "I'm fine."

Nadia held Avaline tighter to her chest. Was her father okay? Was he the one who had made that thudding noise?

Their voices grew hushed and Nadia couldn't hear what they were saying, but a moment later, her mother stepped into the living room. She looked somewhat disheveled, her hair pushed back from her face and sweat beading her clammy skin.

"Hi baby," she said, adjusting the collar of her blouse so that it didn't stick to her skin. She seemed anxious about something, and Nadia didn't like it.

She held up her doll with a smile, hoping to cheer her mom up. "I brushed her hair and she looks so much better," she said.

Her mother forced her lips into a smile, but Nadia could see that her eyes were still shadowed and uncertain. "So much better, honey."

Her mom visibly flinched as they heard another thud from deeper in the house, and a muffled yell from her father. Nadia watched as her mom slowly turned around, her smile fading as fearful tension flooded her features.

"Mom, what's wrong with dad?" Nadia asked in a small voice, clutching her doll again, as though she would find comfort in the familiarity of it.

Her mom didn't respond. Her whole body was coiled tight with fear.

Nadia didn't understand what was happening. Why was her mother so scared, what was with all the banging in the house? Was her father ill?

"Nothing, honey," her mother finally said, but Nadia knew she was lying. *"Your father's fine."*

The memory faded, and a shudder tore through Nadia's body at the surge of emotions flooding her. She couldn't remember what had happened after that, but she knew it had been only a few weeks before that fateful night, when she had come home to her mother's gruesome murder and her father's suicide. Her father had begun acting strange, but she hadn't understood why. Her mother tried to pretend everything was fine, but Nadia knew now that it hadn't been. Her father hadn't just been sick; he'd been possessed by the house and all of its negative energy.

She pulled her knees tight up to her chin, cradling them against her chest. As much as she tried to forget, she couldn't. The house *was* her memory; being back here brought it all up to the surface, and there was nowhere she could hide.

Part of her was screaming to get out of there, to leave it all behind, but she knew she couldn't just run away. Not until they finished the job properly this time. Not until they cleansed the energy for good and put a stop to the horrible tragedies that happened here. Not until she knew for certain that no more families would die here. No more blood would be spilled.

Two figures appeared in the kitchen doorway, snapping her out of her thoughts.

Trish and Amie, toweling off their hands as they took in the solemnity of the room. Like the rest of them, their faces seemed haggard and gaunt in the firelight. Although it was only late afternoon, the house was sunk in its usual shadow, and a chill had sprung up from nowhere, seeping out from the walls of the house. But the fire only did so much to keep the chill and the dark at bay.

Joe shook away his own thoughts and drew his eyes away from the fire to glance at the two in the doorway. His hands fell still in his lap. "You ready?"

Amie nodded, tossing the towel over the back of a kitchen chair and following Trish into the main room. "Ready."

The two women sat down at the table beside Max and Sam, and Nadia pulled the armchair she was sitting in closer towards them, leaving the warmth of the fire behind.

"See anything on the cameras?" Amie asked as Max pulled out an EVP device out of his bag and set it down on the table between them.

Sam shook her head. "Nothing yet."

"Hopefully we'll catch something on the EVP. Something that might tell us why the spirits still remain here."

The others nodded and, after making sure everyone was ready, Max hit the button to start recording.

Nadia forced herself to breathe slowly through her nose, not wanting to worsen the panic thrumming beneath her veins. Now that she was away from the fire, a chill prickled over her neck. She'd never liked doing this EVP sessions, afraid of what kind of answers they would get in response to the questions they asked.

"Is there someone here with us?" Trish started, her loud, clear voice belying the fear in her eyes. The fire had begun to fizzle out now, but nobody made a move to put anymore wood on the flames.

"If you talk into this device, we'll be able to hear you," Sam added softly, gesturing to the small black recorder.

They waited for a moment in breathless silence, and then Joe asked: "Why are you still here? What's holding you here?"

Nadia cleared her throat, shuffling in her chair. She felt the sensation of someone watching her, but everyone in the room had their eyes trained on the table.

Nadia froze, her body going still. For just a moment, it felt like someone had put a hand on her shoulder, long bony fingers digging into her flesh, and a warm breath tickled the back of her neck. Then the sensation was gone, just as quickly as it had happened.

Joe glanced across at her, his gaze questioning, but she ignored him, pulling her legs a little closer to herself. She fought the urge to look behind her, knowing that there was nothing there. Or at least, nothing she would be able to see.

"Did you make Mr. Miller kill his family?" Amie asked, and every eye in the room went to her. She flushed slightly, ducking her head. "What? Might as well get to the point, right?"

The light fixture hanging above them flickered, dimming into shadow before flaring to life again, sending shadows scrambling to and fro. At the same time, a draught blew in from somewhere further in the house, guttering through the fire so that the flames almost blew out, before managing to find a grip on the wood again.

Joe stared hard at the lights. "Well, I think that means we should end the session," he said calmly.

"Yeah, let's stop there," Trish agreed, reaching over to switch off the recording device.

They all sat still and quiet for a few minutes, unwilling to disturb the peace, before Amie straightened up and looked at each of them in turn.

"Sam and Max, you can listen over the audio and see if we caught anything," Amie instructed. "Nadia, you can come with me. I'd like to take a look upstairs with the thermal camera, see if we can get any heat signatures."

Nadia nodded silently, glad to escape this room.

"I think I'd like to take a look downstairs in the basement," Joe added, his voice a low murmur. "In case I can pick up anything at the site of the Millers' murder."

"I'll join you," Trish said, and Joe shot her a glance that she couldn't quite read beneath the shadows on his face.

"Great," Amie said, clasping her hands together. "We'll all meet back up here in an hour and see if we've got anything to share."

Sam and Max stayed where they were, pulling a laptop out of one of their equipment bags and setting it up to listen to the audio, while the others stood from their chairs.

Amie went to grab the thermal camera, and Nadia lingered by the fire in an attempt to fight off the chill she felt, watching Trish and Joe disappear through the kitchen to get to the basement.

Joe walked ahead, his footsteps oddly hurried as Trish struggled to keep pace. He ignored her when she asked what he was hoping to find, not seeming to realize she was there at all.

When they reached the basement door, Joe paused, Trish coming up behind him.

"Hey, you okay?" She asked, touching his arm.

He jumped, looking at her. "Yes, I'm fine," he said shortly, turning back to the door without making a move. He seemed distracted by something.

When he made no move to open it, Trish sucked in a sharp breath and reached forward, wrapping her fingers around the cool metal of the handle. She could feel a chill seeping through the bottom of the door, ruffling the hem of her trousers.

Just as she was about to twist it, Joe suddenly slammed his palm against the wood, preventing it from opening.

"Joe, what the hell!" Trish exclaimed incredulously, but Joe ignored her.

He was listening to something.

From the other side of the door, a female voice was wailing. "Help me…"

Chapter SIX

Nadia went ahead of Amie up the stairs, carrying the thermal camera aloft so that she could watch the screen for any sign of movement.

Part of her shuddered when she remembered the last time she was walking up these stairs, when those invisible hands had reached out from the darkness and shoved her back. She could almost feel every thud and jolt of her body as it hit the stairs, one by one. She was lucky she hadn't escaped with worse injuries. Everything that happened after that seemed hazy, like the memory had shattered into hundreds of pieces and she couldn't quite put them back together again. She'd though it had simply been a result of her fatigue, and the bruises she'd sustained from the fall, skewing with her memory. But after learning that the others had no recollection of it either… it was all so odd. Nothing made sense to her. She had hoped that coming back here would help her and the others recover their memories, but she was still just as confused as before.

As she took the stairs slowly, feeling forward with her toes before stepping down, she focused her attention on the camera. The screen was in shades of blue and green, nothing to suggest anything was giving off any body heat. Every now and then, a small spark of red alerted her places where electric currents were running through the walls.

When she reached the top of the stairs, she sagged in relief. Part of her was expecting to be pushed again, or to lose her footing and fall back. She shuffled forward, hearing Amie sigh behind her, when something flashed across the screen. A heat signature, in the distinct shape of a person; it moved quickly across the screen directly in front of her, before disappearing through the doorway on the left, blinking out of sight

"Did you see that?!" She blurted as Amie came up behind her, looking at the screen over her shoulder.

"No, what happened?"

"I saw something. It looked like a man, but it moved so quickly, I barely got chance to look at it."

"Do you remember anything else?" Amie asked, her voice thrumming with curiosity. "How tall it was, shape, gender, any other details."

Nadia stared hard at the screen, wondering if it would come back. "It looked like a man, taller than either of us. But I… don't remember much else, sorry."

"It's okay," Amie said. "Hopefully we'll see it when we go back over the footage."

"Yeah."

The two of them stepped out onto the landing, and Nadia passed the thermal camera over to Amie so that she could walk ahead, scanning each room.

Nadia lingered back, deciding to try and reach out to any of the spirits lingering there. "If there's someone here with us, could you give us a sign?" She asked, opening her voice up to the house. "The man I just saw. Can you come closer? If you stand in front of that camera that Amie's holding, we'll be able to see you again."

Amie treaded ahead of her. "We won't harm you," she added in a gentle voice. "We just want to talk."

When nothing appeared on the camera, Nadia turned and approached the door on the left, where the man from before had disappeared into. She pushed it gently with her fingertips, and the hinges emitted a loud groan of protest as it swung open.

The curtains were drawn inside, and darkness pooled in each corner of the room. Nadia stepped forward after a moment of hesitation, feeling as though she was about to step into a hole and drop through to the other side.

When she felt the solid floor beneath her feet, she moved forward more confidently. Her eyes took a moment to adjust, staring blindly through the gloom until she began to pick out shapes. She realized she was in her parents' old room. A wave of sadness washed over her, and tears rose unwillingly to her eyes. In her mind, another memory began to play out.

Nadia was sitting at her mother's dressing table, drawing her a picture with crayons. Her mom had seemed distracted lately, and she thought a picture might cheer her up. Humming quietly to herself as she drew, her attention was devoted solely to her work, until something made her start. Footsteps thudded into the room behind her, followed by the sound of someone breathing heavily.

When she looked up in the mirror, her father was standing in the doorway behind her.

Something about him didn't seem right, and Nadia felt a shudder of unease tear through her when she looked at him through the reflection. "Dad?" She said, a faint tremor in her voice. "Are you okay?"

He said nothing, staring motionlessly at her with his hands hanging by his sides. There was a strange sort of haze in his eyes, like he was seeing things from far away, and a pallor to his skin that he only ever got when he was sick.

"S-shall I go and get mom?" She swallowed, her fingers letting go of the crayon so that it thumped to the dresser, rolling away. "Are you not feeling well?"

She twisted around slowly from the dresser to face him behind her. In reality, he looked far worse. Sweat pooled along his brow and his eyes were not just cloudy, but darker in color, completely unfamiliar. Not her father's eyes at all.

"Dad?" She whimpered in a quiet voice. "Please, say something."

He opened his mouth...

And the memory faded, cutting out abruptly like a broken record. She couldn't remember what had happened after that. It had all seemed so long ago. At the time, she'd merely thought her father was ill. Maybe he was stressed from work, or his health wasn't great. Her mom had never said anything about it, so she'd assumed it couldn't have been anything to worry about.

Now she knew what had really happened. If only they'd done something about it sooner. If only they'd got him help. If only they'd left the house and its horrible, negative energies.

Then maybe her parents wouldn't have died. Wouldn't have been *killed*. They would still be here, to see the woman Nadia had grown to be; a successful crime writer, one who wasn't afraid to face her demons.

Back in the present, her eyes readjusted to the room, picking out the space where her mom's old dressing table used to be. It wasn't there anymore, but part of her felt like the memories still lingered, even after all this time. Houses never forgot. Nor did the ghosts that haunted them.

Leaving Amie behind in the hallway, she stepped further into the room, running her hand along the wall. It was damp and clammy, creating a film on her fingers that she quickly brushed away.

It was strange being back here, even if it had changed. It was still her parents' room, and always would be.

She froze suddenly, her hand hovering in mid-air.

For a moment, it had felt like someone had walked past her, stirring the hair against her cheek and crumpling the side of her clothes.

She spun, expecting to see Amie or someone else, but she was alone.

"Mom?" She whispered faintly, her voice reaching out to the dark. "Dad?"

Part of her was desperate for a response. Even the first time they'd come here, they'd been unsuccessful in contacting her parents. She'd only agreed to help them because of the chance of communicating with them, but the only entities they had spoken to were ones of a more malevolent nature. She was beginning to wonder if they were here at all; not all spirits stayed behind, not all energies were strong enough to manifest. But if they were watching her right now, she hoped they knew how much she loved them.

Still standing outside the room, scanning the thermal camera over the hallway, Amie picked up where Nadia left off. "I'd like to ask you a few questions," she said, addressing any spirits that might be lingering nearby. "How old were you when you died? Was this your house?" She let the questions linger for a moment, keeping an eye on the camera in case anything stepped forward. The hallway was empty.

"If you come closer, I'll be able to see you on my camera. It can detect heat signatures," she explained. "If you speak, I might be able to hear you too."

She licked her lips, growing impatient at the silence. "Can you move things? Try touching something." She panned the camera down to a rubber ball that they'd set up in the hallway as a sort of motion detector. If anything brushed past it, the ball was light enough that it would move, but heavy enough not to be stirred by a simple breeze.

"Do you see that rubber ball on the floor? Can you move that?" She said, pointing to the ball.

Nadia retreated out from the room to join Amie, peering at the camera over her arm.

The ball stayed where it was, responding to nothing in the environment, and Amie whistled a sigh. "Looks like we're alone up here," she muttered. "Notice anything in that room?"

Nadia hesitated, then shook her head. The lingering haze of her memories were already starting to fade away, crumbling back to dust in her mind. "Nothing."

Amie turned around, moving towards the door on the right, when her body visibly stilled and she let go of the camera with a stifled yell. The camera thudded heavily against the floorboard at her feet, and Amie stood panting, clearly in shock.

"Amie? What's wrong?" Nadia said quickly, bending down to retrieve the camera from the ground. It still seemed intact, no cracks marring the screen. When she straightened, she looked back at the woman, her eyes darting around wildly. "What did you see?"

"There was someone stood there... right behind me," she said eventually, her fingers trembling as she clutched them to her chest, where her heart was thudding erratically. "It scared me. The heat signature... it was as big as the screen. That's how close they were standing," she said. "Sorry, it just gave me a bit of a fright."

Nadia nodded, moving the camera to look around the hallway. No more heat signatures other than their own.

"I don't see anything anymore," she said. "Whatever it was, looks like it's gone now."

Amie nodded, her body relaxing. "They must have been standing behind me the whole time," she said, the thought making her stomach clench. "I never even felt anything. Not until I turned round and caught them on camera."

Nadia swallowed. "I wonder if it was the same figure as before. The man I saw."

"Maybe," Amie said. Her cheeks were paled, and she still seemed shaken.

"Why don't you go and sit down for a minute?" Nadia suggested gently. "Take a breather."

Amie nodded distractedly. "I think I'll go and get some water," she said, already moving back towards the stairs.

Nadia nodded, but lingered a moment, giving the hallway a final once-over with the camera. She gasped suddenly, calling for Amie to come back.

"Wait, come look at this," she blurted, tugging Amie back to look at the camera, which she had trained on the room she had been standing in before.

On the doorframe was a heat signature in the shape of single a handprint, slowly fading away.

Chapter SEVEN

"Stop!" Joe hissed at Trish, keeping his palm planted firmly against the basement door. "*Listen.*"

Trish snatched her hand away from the doorknob as though she had been burnt, glancing across at the psychic. "What are you hearing, Joe?"

Joe raised a finger to his lips, signaling her to remain quiet as he listened hard to the voice on the other side of the door.

It sounded like a woman's voice, repeatedly begging and pleading for her life. But the sound was distorted, like it was reaching them through water, intercepted by something more than just the door. Joe squeezed his eyes closed, trying to hear anything else beyond the quiet sobs of the woman. Was he hearing some kind of residual haunting? Someone's death repeating over and over, trapped in endless torment.

"I don't hear anything, Joe," Trish whispered impatiently.

His eyes flew open, and he once again gestured for her to be quiet, trying not to lose his concentration. Distractions could easily sever his connection to the other side, which was a fickle thread to begin with.

The woman's sobbing was getting quieter now, as though it was moving further away from them.

He moved closer to the door, pressing his ear right against the wood, ignoring Trish and the rest of his surroundings to focus on what was happening on the other side. He feared that if he opened it, he would sever the thread completely.

As the sobbing got further and further away, no matter how much he tried to call it back, he reached for the handle and tentatively pulled it open, nodding for Trish to move back.

She complied silently, but her features were twisted with a mixture of confusion and curiosity. Whatever Joe could hear, Trish clearly couldn't.

Peeling open the door, he stared down into the darkness pooling at the bottom of the stairs, almost holding his breath. The sobbing had ceased completely, and he couldn't hear anything else but his own breathing.

"Okay, let's go down," he said eventually, taking the first step with Trish close behind.

The stairs were old and rickety, the wood groaning with every step. Joe paused frequently, holding out a hand to stop Trish as he listened to the silence of the basement below. The faintest trickle of water came from somewhere down there, but nothing else.

Trish sighed impatiently, twirling a strand of hair around her finger. The journey down the stairs seemed to take forever with Joe stopping every few seconds to listen. He wouldn't even tell her what it was he was hearing.

The smell of must and mildew swept over them as they reached the bottom of the stairs – but then something else. Something darker, more bitter. Blood.

When Trish's eyes glanced down to the floor, the hair tumbled free from her fingers, brushing gently against her cheek as she let out a gasp.

Joe also went quiet, his lips parted as he stared ahead.

On the ground in front of them, drawn into the cement, were the chalk outlines of three bodies, and the faintest traces of blood left behind.

Trish glanced across at Joe, whose eyes were wide and shimmering with a strange light amidst the gloom. "Joe?" She whispered, her breath hitching. Why was he acting so strange? Ever since they'd come back to the house, she felt like something was off about him.

And now, as he turned to face her with that strange gleam in his eye and a paleness to his cheeks, she knew she was right.

"What's wrong? What are you feeling?"

Joe turned back to the chalk imprints, lifting a finger and pointing towards them. "I can feel them," he said cryptically. "*See* them. The night they died. The night… Mr. Miller killed them all."

"What?"

Joe stepped forward, his hands curled by his side. In his mind, he saw their deaths playing over, the residue of the haunting seeping into him. The knife slashing down, the bloody gashes, a voice begging for him to stop, begging for someone to help. The blood, so much blood, pooling around him, the woman's dying screams.

He could see it all. *Feel* it all. Feel the cold spatter of blood on his skin, the hardness of the knife in his hand. The cries of fear.

"Please, stop. Please don't do this…"

He gritted his teeth, trying to shake it all away. The pain, the fear, the guilt of the realizing what he'd done. The horror that lingered. Years of torment, years of murder.

It was all still here, all still trapped inside the house. Endless. Unforgiven. Unclean.

So many deaths. So many families torn to pieces.

This was a house of murder, where no good things happened.

A house soaked in blood.

"Joe?" Trish said, her voice small and far away.

Joe turned to look at her, blinking away the visions.

"Are you alright? What did you see?"

He stayed quiet. His head was ringing. Remnants of the vision still lingered, obscuring his vision with shades of blood.

"I'm alright," he eventually said, his voice low and hoarse. "I saw their deaths. I… I watched them all die."

Trish swallowed. She didn't know what to say. She knew Joe had a deeper connection to spirits than they did, was able to communicate with them more, tap into their energy. But she couldn't imagine what it must have been like to witness so much death, to see it happening right in front of him.

"Do you want to head back upstairs?" She offered softly.

But Joe shook his head, clenching his jaw. "No. Let's keep going."

Chapter EIGHT

Max took his eyes off the monitor to glance over at Sam. "Catch anything from the EVP session?" He asked. He was snacking on a bag of chips while watching to make sure all the cameras were running smoothly. On the upper right corner of the monitor, the figures of Amie and Nadia could be seen in the upstairs hallway. The rest of the displays were empty, void of any movement.

Sam finished typing something up on the screen and turned to face Max. "I've only just got the audio isolated, but I do see a few peaks where it's caught a voice. I'll let you know more once I've had a listen to it," she said, reaching for the headphones. "Catch anything interesting on the video feed?"

"Nah," Max muttered through a mouthful of chips. "No movement, other than Amie and Trish upstairs. Oh, and a couple of dust mites."

"Hm, well the day's still young. We might get something yet," Sam said before putting her headphones on and hitting play on the audio.

Max's gaze lingered on her for a moment longer as she began to listen to the audio, before he returned his attention to the monitor. So far, he'd barely seen any activity. Like Sam said, it was still early, but given the extent of the energy here, he was surprised they hadn't seen it manifest in more ways.

Even as the thought crossed his mind, something moved on one of the screens.

Dragging his eyes up to the display of the guest bedroom, he noticed that the light fixture had started swinging. The room was empty, and a quick check revealed there were no open windows anywhere upstairs. Something else had knocked it.

Pulling the camera view up onto the whole screen to get a better view, he watched as the light continued to swing on an invisible breeze, moving with increasing urgency and force.

"What the hell?" He muttered, glancing over the rest of the room. There definitely wasn't anyone in there, and nothing could have been causing it to move like this.

He returned to the full display of each cameras, and gasped as a shadow moved across the screen, out of the guest bedroom and out to the hallway, where Amie and Nadia were standing.

Neither of them seemed to notice it.

Max grabbed his radio and clicked it on. "Hey, Amie and Nadia, it's Max. On the screen just now, I caught a shadow moving along the hallway. Can any of you confirm that it was or wasn't you?"

A second later, Amie's voice crackled through. "Neither of us have moved in the past few minutes. Where did you see the shadow?"

"Coming out from the guest room," Max replied, watching the monitor again. The shadow seemed to have disappeared. "It's gone now."

"Alright, thanks for letting us know."

Amie signed off, and Max set down the radio. Things were finally starting to get interesting.

Sam started up the audio they'd captured from the EVP, anxious to see what they'd caught. The sound waves on the computer suggested they'd picked voices up that didn't belong to any of them, and she hoped there wasn't too much interference obscuring the words. Although she'd cleared up as much as she could, the software wasn't fool proof.

Holding the earphones tightly against her head, she closed her eyes to focus on the sounds beyond the soft hiss of static in the background.

After a shuffle of movement, a voice came through; her own, slightly muffled through the recording.

"If you talk into this device, we'll be able to hear you."

A beat of silence passed, and then something interrupted the flow of interference; a low, guttural growl. Followed by a voice, distinctly inhuman, hissing into the recorder: *"It's too late."*

Sam yanked the earphones off her head, staring at Max with wide eyes. The voice had caught her completely off guard.

"What? You hear something?" Max said, reaching forward to take the headphones from her.

Without saying anything, Sam rewound the audio and played it back, bouncing her knee agitatedly as Max listened.

That voice at the end... something about it sent a chill through her. There was something horrifying about the way it spoke, what it said. *It's too late.* What was it talking about? What was too late? The Millers? Or something else?

Max pulled the headphones away slowly, his face scrunched up. "That's creepy. What do you think it meant?"

Sam shook her head, flicking a glance to the corner of the room. "I was trying to figure that out. What's too late?"

Max eventually shrugged, dusting crumbs off his lap. "I guess we won't know. Could be talking about anyone. Even the original owner," he said. "We'll have the others listen to it when they get back, see what they think."

"Good idea."

Sam turned back to the audio device, staring at the screen, still mulling it over. Something bothered her. The more she thought about it, the more she pieced everything together in her head.

Chapter NINE

Nadia brushed her hair out of her face, sweat beginning to pool along her forehead. The air wasn't humid, but her body felt strangely feverish, undulating between hot and cold.

Amie had the thermal camera in her hands, moving it side to side as they explored the rest of the rooms upstairs. Since the figure they had seen standing behind Amie, and the handprint on the doorway, nothing else had caught their attention.

"You know, I was thinking..." Nadia started, drawing the other woman's attention. She stood a short distance away, cupping her chin with her hand as she stared thoughtfully at the floor. "The last time we were here, I don't even remember leaving the house."

Amie blinked at her, her brows casting a shadow over her forehead. "What do you mean?"

"Well, none of us can remember the last day we spent here, right?" She said. "But even leaving and travelling home. I remember none of it. But I have no idea why. Every time I try and think about it, I just feel dizzy."

Amie licked her lips distractedly. "It *is* strange, but I don't have any answers for you right now. That's why we came back, to figure out what happened."

Nadia nodded. "Yeah, I guess you're right," she said solemnly. "I just… it's weird, and a little disconcerting. What really happened that final day?"

Amie said nothing, switching off the camera and lowering it. The same questions had been plaguing her this whole time, but she still felt no closer to piecing it all together. It was possible the house's energy had somehow tapped into their own memories and skewed them, but that didn't seem right either. It was like that last day had never even happened. And the weeks since then… it all felt strange, like a fog was obscuring part of her mind and no matter what she did, she couldn't see past it.

"Amie?"

"Huh?" She glanced up, realizing Nadia was looking at her.

"You alright? You seem a little... out of it," she said with bashful honesty.

Amie nodded, feeling suddenly drained. A wave of fatigue washed over her, and she stumbled back on unsteady legs, trying to reach for the wall but grasping only air. In the shadows, the proportions of the hallway seemed distorted, like the walls were further away than they should be. She shook her head, trying to clear the fog that had settled there.

"Sorry, it's just... I'm starting to feel pretty tired," she said, her eyelids growing heavier and casting a shadow over her eyes as she glanced at Nadia. "The journey always knocks it out of me. I think I might take a nap before we head down to dinner."

"Sure. I guess I'm feeling pretty beat down too," Nadia agreed. "Go get some rest. I'll come check on you in a bit."

Amie nodded and retreated to her room across the hall, while Nadia slipped into her own.

Once inside, Nadia shut the door behind her, leaning back against it with a sigh.

Her body felt strangely heavy. Like Amie had said, it could have been some kind of motion sickness or fatigue from the journey, but this was a sensation that she felt in her very bones, like her energy was completely skewed. The more likely explanation was the house. Being back here was causing her all sorts of discomfort. The memory, the weight of the house's past, it was all bearing down on her like a mountain of bricks, heavy and suffocating.

The suitcase she'd packed hurriedly that morning was sitting at the end of her bed, so she busied herself unpacking the things she'd brought. The bedroom she'd chosen was the old guest room, for which she was glad. She wasn't sure she would have been able to sleep back in her old room or her parent's room. Too many memories. Too much pain overshadowing her childhood.

The clothes she was holding crumpled suddenly in her hands, and she let go, dropping them back into the suitcase with a bitter sigh. Maybe she should finish unpacking later. Her mind was elsewhere at the moment and she desperately coveted rest. Her tired bones, her tired mind. Somehow, she felt like she hadn't slept in weeks.

Throwing the suitcase off the bed, she slid under the covers and sank into the warmth of the sheets, succumbing to her festering dreams.

The darkness was thick around her, almost to the point of being suffocating.

Nadia breathed as quietly as possible, keeping her lips parted as she crawled forward, the floor hard and cold beneath her fingers.

Where was the doorway?

Where were the others?

One moment they were there, then she'd tripped over what felt like a body and now she was alone, crawling through the dark trying to find her way out of the room. Yet the darkness seemed to expand around her, and somehow it felt as though the doorway was getting further and further away the closer she crawled.

She kept moving forward, her knees and arms scraping against the floorboards, but she felt nothing. Just dark, empty space, all around her.

To her right, something moved, and she fell still, her breath falling slack.

Someone grunted softly, and a second later she heard a wet gurgling sound, before something thudded to the floor.

Her heart thudded harshly in her chest. Was there someone in here with her after all?

Swallowing back her fear, she crawled forward with increased urgency, desperate to get out of the room, before whoever lurked in the shadows got her too.

Footsteps pattered behind her, and her movements became panicked, not caring whether or not she made any noise anymore. Her palms slapped against the floorboards and her knees chafed the wood, the darkness parting around her.

A sudden shift in the room alerted her to a wall just ahead. She felt a gentle breeze flowing out towards her, and when she reached her hand forward, she touched the cool plaster of a wall.

Breathing in relief, she began to scramble to her feet, her knees aching as she pushed herself up-

-and then something grabbed her ponytail, yanking her back roughly. Her head snapped back, and in the dark, a face hovered over her, features blurred and indistinct. And then something cold and sharp sliced against her throat, and the darkness became complete.

Chapter TEN

"This is where the Millers died?" Trish repeated as she stared at the basement floor, at the chalk outlines of each body.

Joe nodded, shooting her a furtive glance over his shoulder. His eyes seemed strangely distant, like he was seeing things from far away. Then he blinked, quickly, as though clearing the haze from his eyes. "Yeah, this is where the bodies were found."

Trish tentatively stepped forward, noticing for the first time the traces of blood on the ground. Police had obviously done what they could to clean the crime scene, but remnants remained, stains that couldn't be removed. Dark swathes of reddish-brown in the cement.

She gulped, looking away.

"I'm getting some kind of a vibe from back here," Joe said without looking at her. He wrung his hands together distractedly, stepping over the chalk outlines and moving into the short passageway on the other side of the basement wall.

Trish followed behind him, trying not to stare at the bloodstains as she walked past. On the other side of the passageway was some kind of back room, but Trish's attention remained on the door.

"Look at those locks," she muttered, staring at the four different latches. She reached forward and ran a finger over one of them, smearing the rust that had built up around them. "Why would someone need a door with four bolts?"

Joe shrugged. "Makes you wonder what they kept in here, huh?" He said as Trish pulled her hand away, wiping it down her trousers.

She peered inside but couldn't see much beyond the gloom. There was no natural light down in the basement; only what seeped through from upstairs, which at the moment was limited. She wished she'd brought a flashlight, but Joe had seemed in a hurry to get down here and she'd forgotten.

"Why don't you look inside?" Joe suggested. "I want to take a look at these locks for a minute. I'm curious why anyone would need so many on a single door?"

Trish watched him closely for a minute, picking over the shadows around his eyes and lips. "It's pretty dark in there," she said hesitantly. "Did you bring a light?"

Joe made a show of patting down his pockets before shaking his head. "It doesn't matter. Sometimes it's better in the dark anyway. You can get a feel for the place more."

"I mean, it'll only take a minute to nip upstairs and grab one," she suggested, but her voice died on her throat at Joe's look.

Something really felt wrong with him, but it wasn't something she could put her finger on. He was just acting rather strange, not like he usually did. She tried to tell herself it was because of the house putting them all on edge, but even so, she was starting to worry about him.

"I'll be right behind you," he eventually said, gesturing into the room behind her. She could feel the darkness clawing at her back like something alive, but she pushed back her fear and stepped into the room regardless.

A shiver immediatcly ran through her, goosebumps prickling her skin. It was noticeably colder here than in the rest of the basement, and the air was heavy with damp.

She coughed into her palm as she adjusted to the darkness. It was the sort of damp cold you found in a subterranean atmosphere, under mounds of dirt and soil, moisture seeping through the cracks yet unable to retain any heat.

She rubbed her arms absently, glancing into the gloom around her. It seemed empty for the most part. There was no furniture, no storage boxes. But she felt a jolt of shock go through her when she saw something attached to the wall. Stepping closer, she reached out and touched a finger to the metal chain. It looked like some kind of shackle for attaching something to the wall, or for keeping someone captive…

A soft shuffle of movement behind her made her turn, thinking Joe had followed her inside. But he hadn't. A flutter of dread filled her stomach as she watched the heavy metal door swing closed with a thud, and the hiss of four separate bolts sliding into place, trapping her in there.

As panic rose in her like a tidal wave, and the darkness came alive around her, all she could do was scream.

Chapter ELEVEN

Joe stared at the grooved wood, listening to Trish scream for him to let her out on the other side.

The four locks were engaged, bolted securely across the door. There was no way that Trish would be able to get out. It was designed to keep someone inside, at all costs.

Her screams eventually quietened into faint whimpers, and he felt the smallest stab of guilt in his chest. He knew Trish had to be terrified in there, alone in the dark. He was aware that she'd had bad experiences during her childhood with night terrors and night paralysis, and her fear of the dark had followed her into adulthood too. But he had to do this. This is what he had come back for, after all. This is why he had sacrificed his chance at a future, sacrificed any promise of fame and success. He would not leave without doing exactly what he came here to do.

Now that he had Trish exactly where he needed her, that guilt eventually melted away and was replaced by a feeling of satisfaction. He was already doing what he came here to do. There was no going back now. This was all he had left to complete, then he would be free at last. No more nightmares, no more visions. No more blood and darkness haunting him in the dead of night.

Raising his hand, he rested it against the door, as though he was silently reassuring Trish that everything would be okay in the end. He wasn't doing this to hurt her, but to help her. To help all of them. They'd been his friends, not that long ago. He hadn't forgotten that. But things changed, and sacrifices had to be made.

He turned on his heel and let Trish's cries fade away behind him as he slowly paced across the basement towards the stairs.

With every step, more memories flooded his mind, echoes of the dreams he'd had, reminding him why he was there, why he was doing this.

The blood, the cries, the screams. Each patter and drip of blood hitting the concrete. Those vacant eyes and slack mouths, pale and clammy in death. Fingers curling, reaching for help that wouldn't come, turning drab and grey like stone. And the darkness, creeping towards them all like something alive, something hungry. Whispering to him, mocking him, telling him what he must do.

No matter how much he had tried to forget, he couldn't. Every time he tried to bury those memories, they came back, crawling out from those dark recesses of his mind, begging him to come back and finish what he had started.

So here he was.

Today was the day the truth would come alive.

The day of reckoning.

Chapter TWELVE

Amie stared up at the ceiling, counting every crack that spiderwebbed through the paint. She wasn't sure how long she'd been lying there for. She couldn't even tell how much time had passed since the EVP session with the others downstairs. They were supposed to be reconvening to share what they'd found, but nobody had come to get her yet.

Despite the fatigue still weighing heavily in her bones, she hadn't been able to fall asleep. She felt more drained than she ever had before, almost as though the house was sucking the energy from her and keeping it for itself.

She'd only felt like this once before, at a different house they'd investigated a few years ago. The history there had been even darker, full of lies and deceit and murder. The energy there had been strong, rife with anger and bloodlust, and her own mental energy had been drained because of it. That house had given her nightmares for weeks, after the things she had seen there.

This was different. Hartley House was terrifying in its own way, but she'd never felt like this before. Like her whole body was fading away, crumbling to dust. It was the only way she could describe it. It wasn't just zapping her mental energy, but her physical body too.

Heaving a sigh, she slid out from beneath the covers and swung her legs over the bed, slipping down onto the floor. Her socked feet curled against the carpet as she stretched her arms out behind her, stifling a yawn. Despite how tired she felt, she knew her mind wouldn't be able to rest. Not when so many things were going round in her head. Plus, part of her was worried about the dreams she would have if she did fall asleep. Nightmares were common occurrences in places with bad energy; some of the residual memories and hauntings that had seeped into your mind during the day came alive at night, playing out in your own mind in terrifying visions. A lot of the time, they seemed so real too, as though it was a memory rather than illusion.

She padded into the bathroom, flicking on the light and wincing as the harsh fluorescents burned against her retina. Moving over to stand by the sink, she twisted on the tap and let the water run for a moment, watching it turn from cloudy into a clear stream. Cupping the water into her hands, she splashed it against her face in an attempt to jolt herself awake. Her body still felt sluggish and labored, no matter how much she tried to drive momentum into her muscles.

Blinking the water droplets from her eyes, she glanced up to look in the mirror, and froze.

A figure materialized behind her; at first, hazy and transparent, a blur at the edges of the glass. The it began to solidify, forming features, a face, the body of a woman. A woman who looked *exactly* like herself.

Gripping onto the sink hard enough to turn her knuckles white, she glanced over her shoulder. The doorway behind her was empty; nobody stood there. Yet when she turned back to face the mirror, an exact image of herself stood behind her. Only, it wasn't *quite* her. It was different, somehow. A replica, an imitation. False.

"What… what do you want?" Amie gasped, unable to tear her eyes away from the mirror, from the face that was her own and yet wasn't. A stranger's face.

The figure behind her said nothing. She looked at Amie with dark, deep-set eyes. Shadows crept over her face, dark enough that they almost seemed to swallow her, make her eyes seem sunken, her skin seem transparent. There was blood on the side of her face, caked along her temple, a gruesome reddish-brown.

This couldn't be real. She was seeing things. She must have fallen asleep after all, and this was just some twisted dream, some manifestation of the fear and dread she felt about being back here, back at Hartley House. Surely it couldn't be real…

The reflection behind her raised a pale, slender finger to her lips, giving Amie a devious smile that seemed at once unfamiliar and horrifying. She could never pull off a smile like that, so full of malicious intent, taunting and spiteful.

"What do you want?" Amie repeated, the sharpness of her voice belying the fear that trembled through her. Why was she seeing this? Was the house trying to mess with her mind? Give her horrible visions. Or was it something else?

Still smiling, the figure turned and began to walk out of the bathroom, gliding on silent footsteps. Amie's body went cold with shock and dread as her eyes followed the reflection, seeing the swathes of blood decorating the back of her shirt. And the single, gaping gunshot wound that went straight through her.

Chapter THIRTEEN

Max narrowed his eyes as he watched the camera monitor, moving closer to the screen to get a clearer view of what he was seeing. One of the rubber balls Amie had set up in the hallway upstairs had moved. Only slightly, rolling forward towards the staircase before coming to a sudden halt. He couldn't be certain it wasn't just a draught or the natural slope of the floorboards, but he paid closer attention to the screen in case he caught any more movement.

Sam was still mulling uneasily over the EVPs they had caught in their single session, and while Max also felt disconcerted by the responses, he tried not to let his mind dwell on it. Thinking about it too much would only lead him down a labyrinth of speculation, and he'd learned from experience just to accept things as they were.

A shadow fell suddenly over the tablet screen, dimming the view of the footage.

"What the-"

A hand dropped heavily onto Max's shoulder, and he almost toppled out of his seat with a yelp, making Sam flinch beside him.

"Joe?!" Max blurted as he twisted round in his seat to find the psychic stood behind him, throwing out his hands in defense. "Don't do that! You scared me," he said, gritting his teeth as his heart continued to thud in his chest. He'd barely even heard the man approach them.

"Sorry, sorry," Joe said, his voice unapologetic as he pulled away, shrugging. "I just came to check how things are going."

Max raked a hand through his hair, leaning back in his seat. "Sorry, I didn't mean to yell at you. It's just not cool to sneak up on people in a haunted house, you know?" He added a chuckle, but it sounded weak and strained, and he just as quickly dropped it.

Joe nodded. "Yeah, sorry," he said again, crouching in between Max and Sam. "So, you guys caught anything good yet?"

The two of them exchanged a glance over Joe's head, before Sam nodded hesitantly.

She had the headphones resting in her lap, her fingers tapping nervously against them.

"We've caught a few things from the EVP session," she started, "but… it doesn't really make a whole lot of sense. Max and I thought it was pretty weird."

Joe's brows arched up his forehead, curiosity glimmering in his eyes. "Oh? Can I have a listen?"

"Sure." Sam uncoiled the headphones from her lap and passed them over to the physic, bringing up the audio file on the laptop she was working from. "Give me a second to load it up."

Joe waited patiently, ignoring the strange look Max was giving him from his periphery.

"Okay, take a listen to this."

Joe nodded, slipping the headphones over his ears and shutting his eyes so that he could concentrate better on the audio. Even with most of the interference cleared up, the voices they caught through EVP sessions were often weak and inaudible without the right equipment.

There was a crackle of interference, as though someone was moving, and then Trish's voice speaks through the audio. *"Is there someone here with us?"*

Joe held his breath, waiting for a response.

It came a moment later, the voice low and faint beneath the static. *"The living."*

Joe pressed his lips together, flicking a glance up to Sam's face. Her features were twisted with thought, her eyes unfocused over his shoulder. Max continued to watch him from the side.

"If you talk into this device, we'll be able to hear you."

Almost as soon as Sam spoke, another voice, low and guttural, hissed, *"It's too late."*

At this, Joe started, glancing at Sam again. This time she met his gaze, nodding subtly for him to keep listening.

Joe's own voice seeped through the headphones, distorted through the audio. *"Why are you still here? What's holding you here?"*

"We aren't... you are..."

Joe tugged the earphones off without waiting to see if there was any more left to listen to. "What the hell," he muttered, schooling his features so that the others couldn't quite read his face. The responses weren't quite what he was expecting, but he could see why Sam was so concerned about it.

"There was more too," Sam said irritably as she took the headphones out of Joe's hands, setting them back on the table. She folded her arms together. "At the end, when Amie asks about Mr. Miller killing his family, the same voice as before responds with 'Fake'."

"What do you think it means?" Max asked, watching carefully as Joe's features hardened, his fingers curling in his lap. Something about the way he was acting felt off. He'd noticed it since they'd arrived at the house. He knew everyone was feeling antsy about being back at Hartley, but Joe was… different, somehow. He couldn't explain it.

But even as he watched, the hard solemnity slipped from Joe's features, and his lips curled up into a crooked smile that made Max shiver.

The laptop screen in front of Sam and the tablet in Max's hand went dark, and all the lights in the room flickered, before plunging into complete darkness. Sam whimpered softly, and Max felt his body go cold.

Joe's grin flashed in the dark. A wolf's smile. Hungry and malicious.

"I think it means it's time to end this charade."

Chapter FOURTEEN

Nadia rapped her knuckles lightly against the door to Amie's room, listening out for a response. When Amie didn't answer right away, she gently parted it and spoke through the gap: "Amie? Can I come in?"

She heard a shuffle of movement inside, and then a voice, quiet and subdued against the stillness: "Yes".

Biting down on her lip, Nadia tentatively opened the door and glimpsed inside. Amie was sitting on the edge of her bed, staring out of the window. The curtains were drawn aside, and somehow, dusk had already fallen, bruising the sky a deep purple. The moon glimmered brightly above the rooftops, casting a silver frost along the windowsill. Nadia must have been asleep longer than she thought if it was dark already.

"Did you get any sleep?" Nadia asked, padding slowly into the room. The house was oddly quiet; she could hear no movement from downstairs, no voices or footsteps. It almost felt like the rest of the house was empty, like she and Amie were the only ones there.

Amie shook her head in response to Nadia's question, keeping her eyes on the window even when Nadia sat down beside her, the bed dipping slightly beneath her.

"Are you okay? You seem... troubled by something."

Amie lowered her head. Her fists were curled around the bedsheets, crumpling them around her. When she finally twisted round to face Nadia, her face was cast into shadow, but her eyes were unusually pale and bright, shimmering like the surface of the moon. "I'm not sure."

"What do you mean?" Nadia's voice came out as little more than a whisper.

"I couldn't sleep," Amie started, bringing her knees up to her chin and bridging her hands together, "so I went to the bathroom to freshen up. But when I was in there... I saw something."

"What was it?" Nadia prompted patiently, still speaking in a soft murmur. "What did you see?"

"It was a reflection of myself in the mirror. *Another* me. Only… it wasn't me. Not really."

Nadia swallowed the lump in her throat, bringing her brows together. She didn't quite understand what Amie was trying to tell her. "How so?"

Amie faltered. She sucked her cheeks in, creating deep crevices. "I don't know… Like I said, there was another version of me in the mirror only, it was different. More… frightening." Her voice began to shake, and Nadia reached over to gently touch her shoulder.

"Take a deep breath," she instructed calmly. "Clear your mind. Try and tell me exactly what happened, exactly what you saw."

Amie nodded, sucking a deep breath through her nose before expelling it out through her mouth. Some of the clamminess faded from her cheeks, and she seemed to regain her focus. "Like I said, I went to the bathroom to freshen myself up, and when I looked in the mirror, I saw something behind me. At first, I thought it was some kind of apparition forming behind me. I couldn't really make out what it was at first. But then it began to change into a person, and I realized I was looking at another reflection of myself. I looked behind me, but I could only see it in the mirror. I though it might be a dream, or I was just seeing things, but... but somehow, I knew I wasn't. It was real." She paused to take another shuddering breath, glancing across at Nadia. The other woman gave her an encouraging nod. "She had blood on her face, this other version of me. And something about her just felt off. Like a crude imitation, you know. And then, when she turned and walked out the bathroom, that's when I saw the hole in her back. There was blood everywhere, like she'd been shot." She paused, sniffling quietly, then buried her face in her hands. The next words she spoke came out muffled. "I think she was dead. And I think she was trying to show me the truth."

Nadia said nothing for a moment, trying to find the right words. Part of her knew what Amie was telling her, yet the other half didn't want to believe it. "What truth?" She eventually asked. "You're telling me you think you saw a version of yourself… who was dead?"

"No," Amie said, lifting her head free of her hands and looking at Nadia through blurred vision. "I don't *think* so. I *know* that's what I saw. And it wasn't just a *version* of me. It was me. The *real* me. She was trying to show me the truth."

Nadia chewed nervously on the inside of her lip, shaking her head. "But… Amie, we're in a haunted house. Just because you saw a ghost, doesn't mean it was *actually* you. It doesn't mean it was real. This house plays tricks on the people who stay here. It always has."

Amie gritted her jaw adamantly. "Not this time," she said. "This time, it's trying to show us the truth."

Before Nadia could say anything else, Amie twisted round so that the other woman could see her back… and the gaping, bloody hole of a gunshot wound.

Chapter FIFTEEN

Trish huddled her knees up to her chin, trying to ward off the chill seeping in from by the walls around her. The impenetrable darkness was suffocating, and she could almost imagine things moving around it, reaching for her with long, bony fingers.

She's always been afraid of the dark, ever since she was a child. Even now, as an adult, she still got anxious about being in darkness, often sleeping with a light on to banish those fears that had haunted her since childhood. When she was younger, she would often experience bouts of sleep paralysis. Waking up in the middle of the night, unable to move or speak, while the darkness came alive around her. Hallucinations were common in sleep paralysis, and she remembered figures made of shadow standing over her, pale eyes watching her sleep. The terror she felt, being unable to do anything while those things crept around her bed, was something she still experienced. Although she'd outgrown the sleep paralysis and night terrors in her teens, she'd never been able to shake away that ingrained fear of the dark.

And now, as she pressed her back against the cold cement walls of the basement, those fears felt just as real as they had when she was a child. Her eyes played tricks on her, conjuring creatures out of the shadows. If she listened hard enough, maybe she would even hear the soft patter of feet, the ragged breathing of something watching her from the corner of the room.

She shook the thoughts away, forcing herself not to focus on the darkness around her. She'd already tried searching the room for any possible escape, but the only exit was the door that Joe had shut behind her, the one with the four separate locks. Even her yells and screams had fallen flat against the walls caging her in, and she knew it was hopeless to expect the others to hear here. Down here in the dark, she was alone. And after seeing the shackles on the wall, she was convinced the room was designed to keep someone inside, and not let them out.

She found herself wondering if the room had always been used for such sinister purposes. How many other people had been held captive here at some point in the house's history? How many people had shed their blood down here? Maybe it wasn't just the Millers after all.

Would she die down here too?

Was that why Joe had locked her in there? She didn't understand it. He'd been acting strange all day, but she didn't think he would go as far as doing something like this. Had he been possessed? But surely there would have been some kind of sign. Something to suggest it wasn't really *Joe* doing this, but someone else.

Trish swallowed. Her throat was sore, and her tongue felt heavy in her mouth from the dryness of the air. How much longer would she be stuck down here, at the mercy of the dark and the things that crept inside it?

A sob welled up in her throat, but she pushed it down. She wouldn't cry. Not here, not now, alone in the dark. She wouldn't allow herself. She wouldn't give those eyes in the dark the pleasure of seeing her break down.

She clenched her hands into fists, blinking rapidly as though somehow it would clear the gloom from her eyes.

All of a sudden, a wave of familiarity washed over her. Part of her felt like she'd been here before. In this same darkness, with the cold, dry air and the echoing walls. It was strange, almost like déjà vu, but stronger. It wasn't just a feeling... but a memory.

Blood on her skin, seeping through the material of her clothes. And a face watching her from the dark, a face she knew, and yet at the same time a stranger's face. And a smile like a wolf's, glimmering and pale...

A wave of nausea crept up from her stomach, and she tightened her fists again. What was happening to her? Why did she feel like this? Why was her mind taunting her with such memories, such feelings. Was it the house? Playing tricks on her, planting false memories. She couldn't have been here before. Even the last time they were at the house, she'd never been down to the basement. It was all lies. Just false memories, false feelings.

But where had it come from? Why would the house be forcing her to remember things that weren't real? Were they someone else's memories?

She squeezed her eyes closed, trying to shake away the thoughts racing through her head. She could feel them building behind her eyes in a dull ache.

Shuffling back against the wall, she tried to think of other things. Getting out of there. Seeing her family. It was her niece's birthday soon, and she still had to pick up a present. As soon as she and the others left Hartley House, that's what she'd do…

But the sinking realization that she might not get out at all crashed into her, and she let out the sob she'd been holding in.

Oh god, is this it? All those houses, all those ghosts… is this the one that brings it all crashing down around us? The one house we couldn't beat.

She buried her face in her hands, sobbing quietly. Her head pounded and her body felt heavy with fatigue.

She just wanted to sleep.

She just wanted to escape that darkness around her, and those memories of blood, and the horrible truth that lingered just out of sight. She wanted to sleep, but she was worried even her dreams would provide no respite. If the House was already in her head, then it would follow her wherever she went.

But sleeping was better than waiting, watching the dark. She had no way of knowing how long she would be trapped down there, or if Joe even had any intention of letting her out. She was trapped in the darkness, and the more she focused on that, the worse she felt. Sleep would let it all fade away. Render her invincible to her fears, for just a little while.

Laying down on the cold concrete floor, she rested her head against her hands and closed her eyes, trying to ignore the flutter of anxiety in her chest. She was okay. Nothing could reach her. She was alone down here. Nothing could harm her…

The hiss and thud of a lock disengaging dragged her upright, and her eyes moved through the darkness, trying to find the source of the sound. She couldn't even remember where the door was.

A moment later, after the rest of the bolts had been slid back, the door creaked open and shafts of life poured through, burning against her sensitive eyes. She squinted, throwing up a hand to ease the brightness against her retina, and watched as Joe appeared in the doorway, grinning.

He wasn't alone.

Slumped over his arm was the tall, long-legged figure of Max. He dumped him unceremoniously onto the ground at his feet, pushing him forward with his foot, and then returned with Sam. Trish tried to crawl to her knees, but the frigid air of the basement had stiffened her muscles and she whimpered softly, unable to move.

"Why are you doing this, Joe?" She cried, dragging herself forward on her hands and knees over to Max and Sam. Both of them were unconscious, pale and clammy in the dark. Trish thought she saw blood on Sam's forehead, sticking to her hair.

Joe's figure cast a dense shadow over the doorway, and he suddenly seemed like a stranger to Trish, a stranger in her friend's body. This wasn't the Joe she knew anymore. Whatever the house had done to him, he was changed. She could see it in the way he smiled, the sharpness of his wolfish grin.

The same smile from her vision.

"Why are you doing this?" She repeated more forcefully, the words gritting against her teeth.

Joe cocked his head. His eyes flashed against hers. "Because it's time for you to remember."

Then the door swung closed with another heavy groan, and Trish's heart sank as she listened to the four locks click back into place.

Chapter SIXTEEN

Nadia's breathing stalled as she stared at the wound on Amie's back, the blood gleaming wetly in the moonlight. "What the hell happened?" She gasped, subconsciously bring out her hand to reach forward. Her fingers hovered inches from Amie's back, before she quickly recoiled, snatching her hand back against her chest.

"I told you," Amie said, turning so that Nadia could not longer see the hole that had torn through her body. Her skin was even more ashen than before, almost bone white. "I'm dead. *We...* are dead."

Nadia shook her head adamantly. "No, we can't be. This has to be a dream." She fought back a surge of bile, feeling sick to her stomach. Amie didn't know what she was saying. She couldn't. It didn't make any sense. How could they be dead?

"Nadia, listen to me," Amie hissed, grabbing her by the shoulders, but Nadia shook her away, breathing heavily.

"It's the house," she said, her voice rising almost hysterically. "The house is messing with you, with *us*. None of this is real."

Amie's face remained solemn, hard. And Nadia knew she wasn't lying. Deep down, she knew that Amie was right.

Trembling, she slowly reached up and pressed a hand against her throat. When she pulled away, her fingertips were covered in dark, wet blood. A surge of dizziness hit her, and she swayed for a moment, her mind racing in shock and denial.

"Can you feel it now?" Amie whispered, her voice more defeated than angry. "Do you believe me?"

Despite the overwhelming urge to deny it, to continue under the belief none of this was real, Nadia nodded. Her body was starting to feel strangely light, like she was beginning to fade away, a painting mixed with too much water.

The faint sting of her throat, the blood, the gurgling quality of her words. The truth was right in front of her. "My throat," she whispered, and a trail of blood dribbled down from her lips. "It's... it's cut, isn't it?"

Amie looked away sadly. "Go and look in the mirror. It'll show you the truth."

"No," Nadia said. "I don't want to see it. Just tell me."

"Yes." The single word was like a bullet, punching Nadia in the gut so that she was forced to curl over, pain blooming through every nerve in her body.

Tears blurred her vision, and she let them fall, mixing with the blood on her skin.

"I'm really dead?" She sobbed. "We're all dead?"

But how could it be possible? This whole time – had it been nothing but a lie? An illusion? A cruel twist of fate. Hartley House had the last laugh after all. It had finished the job, severed Nadia's bloodline. Of course, Harley House left no survivors. Anyone who lived there was doomed from the start. There was no chance of escape, no chance of surviving. Nadia had believed the lie for eleven years, but in the end, the ghosts always won.

"It's not fair," she sobbed, her whole body shaking. Even the moon seemed to taunt her, grinning over the rooftops. "It wasn't supposed to end like this. We were supposed to cleanse the house, we were supposed to stop anyone else from getting hurt."

Amie said nothing. She let Nadia grieve. She'd come to terms with the truth since seeing the reflection in the mirror, the only real part of all of this. The mirror had broken the illusion, shown her what was real and what was not. Shown her the fate they had all succumbed to, on that fateful last day.

Blood and death. Murder and suicide. Tragedy.

That was the truth of Hartley House.

Chapter SEVENTEEN

Joe grinned as he made his way upstairs, his arms swinging absently by his side.

Three down, two to go, he thought. *Then it's all over. I can finally show them the truth. And I can put an end to all of this.*

When he reached the door to Amie's room, already partially ajar, he pushed it open the rest of the way and strode inside without waiting for an invitation.

The two women were sitting side by side on the bed. When Nadia turned to look at him, he saw the tears glistening on her cheeks, and the blood smeared around her throat. Amie's back was a mess of blood and torn skin, and the material of her shirt was soaked crimson.

Joe's smile dimmed beneath their stares. *They already know.*

Neither of them spoke for a few minutes, until Joe eventually broke the silence. "You two need to come with me," he said, his voice harsh and unyielding. He saw Nadia flinch, but Amie's face only tightened, her eyes thinning.

"Why?" She said, her voice just as hard.

Joe curled his hands into fists. "Because the others need to realize what really happened to them. And I need your help."

"How can we?" Nadia said. She sounded defeated, another stray tear leaking from her eye. "Even I don't know what really happened. All I know... All I know is that we're dead."

"Not all of us," Joe muttered, cocking his head to the side in almost playful manner. "If you don't help me, then they won't be able to move on. You'll all be stuck here, living in endless torment, just like all of those other spirits. You'll be nothing more than a voice amongst the static, a shadow out of the corner of someone's eye."

His words struck them both with the weight of truth, and the two women exchanged a sad glance.

"He's right," Amie said eventually. "We'll all be stuck here, just like the other victims. Reliving our pain over and over again."

Nadia swallowed, staring down at the floor, and after a moment, she nodded. "Okay," she said, facing Joe again. The tears had dried on her cheeks, and she hastily brushed the hair out of her eyes, smearing blood and sweat. "We'll help them. But we're doing this for them. Not for you."

Without another word, Joe turned on his heel and strode out of the room.

Amie and Nadia stood together, and Amie gave her a comforting squeeze on the arm before the two of them followed Joe out of the room.

The house was deathly silent. Now that Nadia looked closer, she could see that the house hadn't changed at all. There were no new carpets or new furnishings. It had all been an illusion, a lie. The dirt was still there; the dust and the grime and the blood, old and new stains. They had been here all along, and they just couldn't see it. The House had tried to hide from them, disguise its true nature under a façade, but it had been there all along.

Amie walked beside her, her head bowed to stare at the floor, and Joe went on ahead, barely sparing them a glance to make sure they were following.

Nadia was still trying to wrap her head around everything. *Dead. I'm really dead. These past few weeks… they've all been a lie. I never left Hartley. I've been here all along.*

In a way, she supposed she was always destined to die here. She should have died along with her parents eleven years ago, but some lucky – or cruel – twist of fate had thrown a wrench in those plans, and she'd escaped.

But in the end, Hartley House left no survivors. That's just the way it was.

She was angry though. Angry at the unfairness of it all, the injustice. She might have been destined to die here, but the others weren't. They had nothing to do with Hartley. They shouldn't have been caught up in this mess, this *curse*. None of them deserved to die.

She knew that the Joe walking ahead of her wasn't the same Joe who she'd met all those weeks ago. The House had gotten into him somehow. He was nothing more than a puppet, just like her father had been when he murdered his own wife – Nadia's mother – in cold blood.

Just like her father, Joe had been vulnerable to the House's energy. He'd been an easy target, with his deeper connection to the spirits. They were merely using him to do their bidding, to continue the curse that had given the house such a dark and gruesome history.

But that didn't make it any easier to accept. In the end, nobody should have had to die. Not her parents, or Amie and the team. Not any of the families who came before them.

The House was unnatural. A place of darkness. Instead of trying to cleanse it, they should have just shut the place up for good. That way, nobody else would have gotten hurt.

With Amie beside her and Joe ahead of her, Nadia began to succumb to her memories. They were tugging restlessly at her.

The silence, the smell of blood, the shadows… it was exactly the same as that night. The night that changed her life forever, that would keep her coming back here, even so many years later.

Because Hartley House didn't let go, not so easily. She was never supposed to leave this place alive.

And all of a sudden, she was a child again. Eleven years ago, coming home early from a sleepover because of the impending sense of dread that she felt. Coming home to that strange, unnatural silence, to the shadows that seemed more alive than usual, more sinister…

Nadia walked forward, her pajamas sticking to her clammy skin as she reached out with her fingers to feel the walls either side of her.

The house wasn't usually this dark. Wasn't usually this quiet. Where had everyone gone? Where were her parents?

I'm home… Mom? Dad? Where are you?

A chill crawled over her arms, burrowing deep into her bones. The air was cold, heavy. Like the air in the basement, whenever her mom sent her down there for cleaning supplies or her dad's toolbox. She hated it down in the basement, with its cold grey walls and dozens of cobwebs, all hanging down from the ceiling. She would always linger for ages at the top of the stairs, unwilling to take the first step, afraid of what waited in the dark. And the room at the end of the basement, the one with the four locks… the room her parents had forbidden her to enter.

She shook away the memories, creeping forward through the darkness until she reached a door.

She paused. This wasn't the living room door, like she thought she was heading towards. This door led down to the basement.

What was she doing here? Why would her parents be down there? Isn't that who she was looking for?

Even though it made no sense, she found herself reaching forward, wrapping her fingers around the cold handle and pulling it open.

Darkness stretched out in front of her, thickening into something tangible. She couldn't see the bottom of the stairs. She could barely even see her own outstretched hand.

What was waiting for her down there?

Where were her parents? What was she doing here?

Nothing made sense, and yet she was driven by an overwhelming urge to keep moving forward. That was all she could do. Keep walking, until things made sense again. Until she found the truth.

Staring down into the gloom, she took the first step, inching forward with shuffling movements. The wood groaned beneath her like the sound of creaking bones, and she worried for a moment that it wouldn't hold her weight, that it would collapse beneath her and send her sprawling into that darkness.

As she made her way further down, she became aware of the growing smell of blood. It was a strangely familiar scent, dredging up memories she had forgotten.

Blood. So much blood.

Where had it all come from?

The nearer she drew to the bottom of the stairs, the stronger the smell became, until it was almost overwhelming, making her feel faint.

Was someone hurt down here? Did someone need my help?

Despite the fears tearing through her, the nausea roiling in her stomach, she kept going.

Whatever was waiting for her at the bottom, she would face it head on.

When she reached the bottom, the darkness seemed to part just enough for her to see. The glistening wet patches on the ground. The shapes in the darkness.

Bodies.

There were bodies here. She counted six in the darkness, but part of her knew there were more. Lying just out of sight. Just out of reach. That's why it smelled so strongly of blood.

There had been a massacre.

Her feet landed in something wet and slippery, and she almost fell, sliding forward and kicking something that crunched softly beneath the impact.

A body. She'd kicked a body.

Crouching down to her knees, the soft material of her pajamas cushioning her from the cold floor, she reached forward and brushed aside the hair that was covering their face.

It was a woman, with blonde hair and blue eyes, glazed over with death. Blood trickled down the side of her face, her mouth locked open in a horrible scream.

Somehow, she recognized her. She knew this woman, and yet... she couldn't remember why. Where had she seen her before?

Then a name came to her lips. A name that she knew belonged to the woman in front of her.

Amie.

She turned away from the body, looking across the floor and saying each name in her head as her eyes fell across them.

Trish. Sam. Max.

All familiar names, familiar faces. All hidden beneath swathes of blood and shadow.

All dead.

Further away, at the back of the room, two more bodies lay together, gleaming with blood.

Her chest ached when she saw them. The ones she had been looking for this whole time. They were here, waiting for her in the dark. Waiting for her to join them.

Mom… Dad… I'm-

"-home…"

Amie turned to Nadia, surprise flashing across her face. "What was that?"

Nadia blinked, the memories crumbling to dust before her. None of that had been real… she was imagining it all. Yet she knew the truth had been buried in there somewhere. "Nothing, sorry," she muttered, glancing around.

She and Amie were standing behind Joe at the top of the basement steps. A cold, damp breeze washed up to meet them, and for a second, Nadia could smell the blood from her memory. Or was it real this time?

A pang of dread twisted her stomach as she stared down at the darkness, wondering for the last time what lay waiting for her at the bottom.

"You ready?" Joe said, flashing a smile over his shoulder, before taking the first step forward.

Chapter EIGHTEEN

"Max! Sam!" Trish hissed, her voice dampened by the walls bearing around them. "Are you two awake?"

Ahead of her, someone grumbled quietly in pain, and she heard the shuffle of someone struggling to sit up.

"Barely," Max grunted, breathing heavily as he rubbed the back of his head. "Where the hell am I?"

"We're in the basement," Trish said, crawling forward on her hands and knees as she searched for the others, gritty cement cutting into her palms. Her hands came into contact with something soft, and Sam winced in pain.

"Ouch!"

"Sorry," Trish whispered, pulling away. When she focused her eyes, she could just make out the outline of two people in front of her.

"In the basement?" Max echoed, his voice tight with incredulity. "Why? What's going on?"

"Joe locked us in here," Trish said, swallowing thickly. The air was starting to make her throat feel itchy, and her voice came out dry and hoarse. "I think he must be possessed or something. Something's not right."

"No kidding," Sam said, groaning quietly again. Every movement of her head sent a new wave of pain through her. "He hit me over the head with something. Now it hurts like hell."

"Is there a way out of here?" Max's voice floated out of the dark, sounding further away than before. Trish tried to keep sight of him, but it was difficult in the dark.

"Stay close," she said. "And no, I already checked. The only exit is the way we came in. The door that Joe locked behind him."

Max swore softly, and Sam heaved a sigh. Trish heard more shuffling ahead of her.

"How long do you think he'll keep us down here? And what's he planning on doing to us?"

Trish shrugged dejectedly. "Your guess is as good as mine," she said. If Joe really was possessed, why would he lock them up down here? He must have something planned. "I felt like something was off with him since we got here, but I never thought he'd do something like this."

"Do you think… do you think he's going to kill us?" Sam asked, her voice small and shaky in the dark. "Are we going to die down here?"

Trish shook her head adamantly, but even she wasn't so convinced. If Joe really was possessed, there was only a very slim chance he would let them all go. If the House got its way, none of them would be leaving alive.

She felt forward again and found Sam's hand, squeezing it gently. "Don't think about those things," she said. "Maybe we can reason with him."

Trish saw Sam nod, her eyes glimmering with fear as she stared at her through the gloom.

"Max? Where did you go?"

"I'm here," his voice came a second later, to the left of them. "Just looking around."

"There really isn't much to see," Trish said dryly. "Come back over here so we know you're alright."

With a reluctant sigh, Max stumbled back towards them, almost tripping over Nadia's legs.

Trish felt better with the others around her. Although the darkness still hid what was waiting for them, at least she knew she wasn't alone now.

As she sat mulling over their options, the familiar sound of four locks disengaging drew her attention.

Max and Sam went quiet too, watching as the door slid open and a faint square of misty light cut through, illuminating a few meters into the room.

Trish shielded her eyes, noticing for the first time that Joe wasn't alone. Amie and Nadia were stood either side of him, only they seemed strangely pale and distant, as though she was seeing them through some kind of broken lens.

Then she saw the blood. Nadia's throat was slashed to pieces, shadows and blood mingling around her skin, and Amie had something dark and wet trickling down the side of her head.

What the hell was going on? How was Nadia still alive with a wound like that, and what had happened to Amie?

Even in the gloom around them, Trish saw Joe's playful smile, watching the three of them like a wolf watches a rabbit, blissfully unaware of its fate.

"What are you doing, Joe?" Max demanded, his voice hard. "Let us out of here."

Joe cocked his head. "Sorry, Max, but I can't do that."

"Yes, you can, Joe. Just let us go. We can all get out of here. Nobody else has to get hurt."

Joe's smile faded, and he shook his head. "You don't get it, do you? You're never leaving this place again."

Amie and Nadia lowered their gazes to the feet, as though they knew more than they were letting on. Trish couldn't take her eyes off Nadia's neck, the blood spilling out from the gash. Nothing she was seeing made sense.

"Joe, tell us what's going on. Why are you doing this?"

The psychic's smile returned, widening into something malicious and unnatural. "I'm trying to help you," he said. "I want you to remember."

"Remember what?" Trish managed to croak out, dread weighing like a stone in her stomach.

Joe's teeth flashed.

"To remember how you all died."

Chapter NINETEEN

The silence was palpable, crashing over them like a tidal wave.

Dead. They were all... dead?

But how could that be? It wasn't possible. Here they all were, flesh and blood, still breathing, still living.

Yet, as they glanced amongst each other, the terrifying revelation hit them all one by one, and the memory of that last day that had been so elusive finally revealed itself.

Max couldn't see anything.

He couldn't hear anything.

Were the others still here? Was he alone? He didn't understand what was happening. Joe had blown the candles out and Sam had screamed, and there'd been something watching them from the corner of the room, something with an inhuman growl and long, tapered claws.

And then everything had gone silent.

He moved forward, panic thrumming in his veins.

He could hear someone crawling, the soft scrape and thud of knees, feet, being dragged forward. But he didn't know who it was. He couldn't even form the words to ask, afraid it was neither of the others, but something else…

Max froze suddenly as something tickled the back of his neck – a breath. Before he could shout or turn, a hand came out of the dark, connecting hard with his head and sending him spiraling even deeper into that darkness.

Amie found the door first. The others must have still been, behind her, stumbling blindly through the darkness, though she couldn't hear them. Feeling across the wall, she searched for the light switch, her fingers finally finding it with a glimmer of hope. But when she tried to turn it on, nothing happened. The darkness was unbroken.

Cursing softly beneath her breath, she slipped out through the door into the kitchen. Even with the windows uncovered, there was only darkness. No moon or stars. Even they had abandoned them tonight.

A figure appeared ahead of her, breaking away from the shadows to stand in front of her.

"J-Joe?" She stuttered, relief flooding her. "I'm so glad you're okay. I thought you'd gone… Joe?" Her voice faltered when she saw the gun in his hand, gleaming wickedly in the glint of his eye. "Joe, what are you…" When he lifted the barrel of the gun directly towards her, she turned and started to run. She'd glimpsed the madness in his eyes, and knew with cold certainty that he would shoot her without hesitation.

The first bullet hit her in the back. Pain exploded across her body, and she fell forward with a wet, gurgling grunt.

The second one grazed the side of her temple, but by that point, she was already dead.

Sam's leg stung with each movement. Whatever had scratched her had had fingers like claws, raking right through the material of her pants and cutting into the skin beneath. Warm blood trickled down her leg, but she couldn't even see enough to know the extent of the wound.

She grunted quietly as she limped forward, her fingers outstretched as she tried to find the way out of the room. Her mind was spinning with confusion, trying to process what was happening.

Where had Joe gone? Where were the others?

She could see nothing, hear nothing. It was almost as though she was being smothered by the darkness; it coiled around her like something alive, muffling her steps and blinding her vision.

She heard a voice somewhere ahead of her – female, familiar. Amie. Dragging her injured leg behind her, she moved forward with increased urgency, desperate to get to the other woman...

A gunshot blasted ahead of her, one, then another, sending her ears ringing.

She choked out a cry, blinking rapidly to see what was happening in front of her.

A gun? Who was shooting at them? What the hell was going on?

"A-Amie?" She cried. "Amie, are you there?"

Her foot connected with something on the ground in front of her and she fell, landing on her knees. Pain tore through her leg, more blood welling to the surface of her skin, and she felt forward with trembling hands, her fingers brushing something soft and bristly. Hair.

"M-Max? Oh god, Max, are you okay?" She gasped, finding his shoulder in the dark and trying to shake him awake. "Max! Max, please wake up."

Footsteps fell ahead of her, and she looked up as a figure emerged in the dark, grinning devilishly.

Joe.

He lifted the gun and sent a bullet into Max's body. He jerked, one final breath shuddering out of him before he fell still.

Sam screamed, scrambling away desperately from Max's unmoving body and the blood begin to spread around him. "Joe, no. What are you doing? Stop! Please, stop."

Joe turned the gun on her without hesitation, without remorse. In the dark, the barrel gleamed with a wicked light.

He aimed it right between her eyes… and pulled the trigger.

Trish remembered waking up in the dark, her skull pounding, pain blossoming through her body. When she reached out to touch her stomach, she pulled away with blood on her fingers, wet and sticky, still fresh.

What was going on? Why was she bleeding?

The last thing she remembered was the séance, the candles blowing out, leaving them in darkness. She'd tried to find the way out, tried to get the lights back on, but somehow the darkness had tricked her, led her astray.

Then… pain. Pain all over her body. She'd felt a knife cut through her, twisting in her gut, blood spilling out.

Someone had stabbed her. Someone she knew.

And then she'd woken up in this damp-smelling, cold, impenetrable darkness. The floors were cement, rough against her skin, and the air was heavy, stifling. Like she was underground somewhere.

The basement?

But how did she get down here? Why couldn't she remember what happened?

The pain in her stomach was getting worse by the minute. She was losing too much blood. She could feel it pooling around her, making the ground slick and sticky.

And she realized, with startling certainty, that she was dying. Without any medical help, the wound was fatal. She would be dead in a matter of minutes.

She was alone, in the dark - that same dark she had been terrified of as a child - and she was bleeding to death.

Nadia breathed heavily. She was on her knees, next to a body. The body she'd tripped over on her way to the exit. She knew she had to get out of there, out of the dark, but she couldn't. She was struggling to breath. Struggling to think. Her body wouldn't move.

The body... whose body...

She reached forward through the darkness, knowing that it lay right behind her. Part of her knew what she would find, yet she had to know, she had to be certain.

Her fingers found the hair first, long, limp strands of it. Even though it was dark, she could picture it clearly. Long blonde hair streaked with blood.

"Mom..."

This was where she had found her, eleven years ago. Lying on her back near the doorway between the living room and the kitchen, in a puddle of her own blood, her body torn to shreds.

A twelve year old child, losing both parents in the same night, losing them to the darkness that had been living beneath their noses the whole time.

Nadia sobbed quietly, pressing her fingers to her mom's cold cheek. The skin felt stiff and clammy beneath her touch, and she could see the hazy veneer of her mom's eyes, staring at her lifelessly.

"Oh, mom," she whispered, her voice choked with sobs. "Why did it have to happen like this? Why did you have to die?"

Eleven years since that night. Eleven years of battling self-guilt, the regret of not being there to stop it from happening. Eleven years of nightmares, of anger and dread and fear. Eleven years of loneliness.

She hated Hartley House, and yet she always found herself coming back.

Somewhere in the darkness around her, someone grunted softly in pain, followed by the thump of a body hitting the floor.

Nadia held her breath. She wasn't alone. She had to move, had to find a way out of here.

Keeping as quiet as she could, she left behind the body of her mom and crawled forward. The door should be right ahead of her. Yet even as she kept crawling, she felt nothing. Where was the door? Was there no end to this darkness?

Nothing but empty space, billowing around her, taunting.

You can't leave, it seemed to say. You're home now. And we're never letting you go.

Footsteps pattered behind her, and her movements became panicked, not caring whether or not she made any noise anymore. Her palms slapped against the floorboards and her knees chafed the wood, the darkness parting around her.

A sudden shift in the room alerted her to a wall just ahead. She felt a gentle breeze flowing out towards her, and when she reached her hand forward, she touched the cool plaster of a wall.

Breathing in relief, she began to scramble to her feet, her knees aching as she pushed herself up-

-and then something grabbed her ponytail, yanking her back roughly. Her head snapped back, and in the dark, a face hovered over her, features blurred and indistinct. And then something cold and sharp sliced against her throat, and the darkness became complete.

Dead. They were all dead.

Joe had murdered them all, just like so many others before him had murdered their families in cold blood.

"I don't understand," Trish whimpered, clutching her stomach. Blood stained the front of her shirt, in the same place she'd been stabbed. This cold, damp basement room was where she'd bled out, waiting for the darkness to take her. "Why did you do it?"

Joe laughed. It was a chilling laugh, containing no warmth, no emotion. An inhuman laugh. "There is no *why*," he said, his voice heavy with mocking. "It was what the House desired. And it chose *me* to do its bidding."

"But why did you come back?" Nadia asked, her voice a low, trembling whisper. "Why put us all through this?"

Joe sobered, his eyes shadowing with pain. "I was never meant to live in the first place," he said solemnly. "After I killed you all, one by one, I dragged your bodies down here to the basement and went upstairs to call the police. I'd intended on shooting myself right then, before the police arrived, but I'd misplaced the rest of my bullets." He gave another bitter laugh. "The police arrived sooner than I expected. They didn't give me chance to shoot myself, to finish the job, so I had to play along with it. An intruder in the house, killed all my friends, blah blah." He shook his head, leaning against the door. "I thought maybe I could leave all this behind me. I tried to move on with my life, enjoy my newfound fame as a high-profile psychic, but this place… it doesn't let you forget it. It was in my dreams, in every waking thought. I couldn't eat, couldn't sleep. Every part of me was yearning to come back here. To *finish the job*. So you see, I *had* to come back. I had no choice. The House leaves no survivors."

"But… the Millers? Was any of that real?" Amie whispered from beside him, her face deathly pale.

"No," Joe said bluntly. "It was all a lie. It was the only way I could bring you all back here, to show you the truth. I made it all up, about the house being sold, the new family moving in, their tragic deaths, murdered by their own father and husband in the basement. It wasn't them who were really killed." He looked at them each in turn, their pale, ashen faces, the blood and the tears, the expressions of grief. He sighed. "But like I said, it's not over yet," he said sadly, reaching into his back pocket and pulling out a gun. The same one he'd used to shoot his friends.

"What do you mean?" Sam asked, her voice trembling.

"The House doesn't leave survivors," he echoed. "Nobody gets out of here alive. I have to finish what I started."

"Wait, Joe, you don't have to do this. You don't-"

Nadia squeezed her eyes closed as the gunshot shattered the darkness around them, and Joe joined the rest of them in death.

Blood and death. Murder and suicide. Tragedy. That was, and always had been, the truth of Hartley House.

Epilogue

"Tragic news today in Albion County," the reporter said, levelling his gaze with the camera that was broadcasting him live to the local news station. Hartley House loomed behind him in the background, blotting out the mid-morning sun and casting a shadow over the camera crew. "Joseph Dunlap, the newest high-profile psychic, committed suicide late last night here at Hartley House."

He paused, turning to glance up at the building, with its grimy brown bricks and tumbling ivy, its vacant windows, watching him like shadowy eyes. The camera moved forward as he began picking through the wiry brown grass, towards the front door. Police caution table crisscrossed the porch, vivid and bright against the shadows lingering in the doorway.

The reporter turned back to the camera, unable to hide the shiver of unease he felt at having the house at his back. Even despite the reports he'd read about the place, he wasn't a believer of the supernatural. But now that he was here, with the House in his view, even he couldn't deny the prickle of dread it gave him.

"Joseph was the lone survivor of the recent tragedy that happened here, several weeks earlier, when the paranormal investigation team he was part of were found murdered in the house's basement." He paused again to swallow, the words sticking in his throat. "The motives for his suicide have yet to be determined, but given the house's connection to his team, there has been a lot of speculation."

He lifted his gaze again, glancing over the vacant windows as if expecting to see a face peering back at him. "Some have speculated that, even though his name had been cleared as a suspect in the initial murders, this could lead to the revelation that he was not so innocent as he seemed, and did in fact have a hand in the crime. Others pay special attention to the history of the house, and the long string of murder-suicides that have happened here over the years. One of Joseph's team members who were murdered here was Nadia Owens, the survivor of another tragic murder that happened here over eleven years ago. It feels an awful lot like history is trying to repeat itself."

With a mystifying expression, he made direct contact with the camera again, feeling the cold shadow of the house against his back. "So I'll leave you with this: was Joseph Dunlap's suicide the result of survivor's guilt, for being the only one left of his team to make it out alive that night? Or was it the result of guilt for having a hand in the murder of five innocent people. *Or* was this simply the outcome of the long-standing curse of Hartley House that has remained unbroken, even to this day? Until we get more details from the police running the investigation, I'll let you decide."

"This is Tom Harven, signing off."

THE HAUNTING OF REDBURN MANOR

SNEAK PEAK

(Available on Amazon now)

Chapter ONE

The car skidded to a stop with a sudden lurch, and something thudded against the floor of the trunk. Avery jerked forward in her seat, catching herself against the headrest in front of her, and shot John, their driver, a narrow look.

The man smiled sheepishly, brushing a piece of curling grey hair away from his face. "Sorry," he said. "Hope none of your equipment got damaged."

"I'm sure it's fine," Nathan said with a dismissive wave, unclipping his seat belt. "Thanks for the ride. You remember when you're picking us up?"

"End of the week," John said. "Friday."

Nathan nodded and reached over to open his door. In the back, Randall, Lucy and Avery groaned and stretched as they shuffled out of the car. They'd spent the two hour car journey squashed together with their luggage that couldn't fit in the trunk.

Avery stretched her arms over her head, hearing her shoulder joints pop. "Glad that's over," she muttered, going round the back of the car to help Randall unload the bags.

Nathan propped his hands on his hips with a mystified look on his face. "I thought the journey was fine. Pretty comfy if you ask me."

The three of them shot him a look, and he cowered with a grin. "Alright, alright, you can fight over the front seat next time."

Hauling their bags onto the pavement beside the car, Randall shut the trunk and they waved John off as he pulled away, saluting them in the wing mirror.

"Well, this is it," Lucy said. "We're here."

Nathan nodded at the house in front of them. "Redburn Manor, in all her beauty."

"More like fallen splendor," Lucy muttered, scanning her eyes over the grimy brown bricks, spiderwebbed with cracks and dirt. Ivy tumbled down one side of the house, pushing through the bricks with its long, spindly tendrils.

"There's a certain charm to it," Randall said with a shrug. "What do you think, Avery?"

The three of them turned to her, and she dragged her eyes away from the upper window, where she'd been staring. "Charming, yeah," she said distractedly.

"Well, shall we get inside then?" Nathan said, producing an old-fashioned key from his pocket.

"Lead the way."

It was already late in the afternoon by the time they'd arrived at the house, and although the air was warmed from the sun, grey clouds were banking in from the west, burgeoning with rain, and a chill had begun to blow, stirring leaves across the pavement.

Redburn Manor was a shadow blotted against the sky. An old, crumbling husk of something that was once grand and beautiful. It was a three-story building, with ornate turreted windows that now seemed drab and gloomy in the shade, the glass dirty and cracked in places.

As Nathan slid the key into the lock, Avery almost held her breath.

The door opened without a noise. Particles of disturbed dust flew up, glinting in the wavering light of the afternoon. Nathan shot the others a glance over his shoulder before being the first to step inside. Randall followed, then Lucy.

Avery waited another few seconds before she too stepped forward. From where she was stood, the entryway stretched down into semi-darkness. The sunlight that had been warming her back before dipped behind one of those dark clouds, and the wind stirred strands of hair across her face.

"You coming?" Lucy asked, glancing over her shoulder when she noticed Avery hadn't followed.

Schooling her features into a more casual pose, she nodded and stepped in after them.

The sensation of dust on her skin was the first thing she noticed; it itched along her arms and tickled the back of her throat, making her cough. The place had been shut up for a long time, after its last stint as a Bed and Breakfast a few years ago. After the last tragedy happened, the place sunk into its own despair, becoming a place nobody cared for anymore.

"Woah!" Randall said from further inside. "This place is huge!" His voice echoed along the high-vaulted ceiling, stirring the cobwebs that latticed the rafters. There was a staircase on the left, which stretched up into darkness, and on her right, an old-fashioned mirror with gilded edges that was obscured by dust and old fingerprints.

Lucy ran a finger along its edge, pulling away a streak of muck.

"Back when it was a Bed and Breakfast, this place was able to accommodate up to twenty people," she said as she used the sleeve of her jacket to wipe away some of the dirty prints on the glass. Avery watched the reflection clear, showing her the staircase on the opposite side. Mirrors were often said to hold a lot of spiritual energy, and she made a note to keep an eye on it.

"I thought it was a hotel?" Randall said.

"That was before it became a Bed and Breakfast. Neither businesses lasted very long."

"And before any of that, it served as a mental institution," Nathan added, his teeth flashing in the dark.

The rest of them shared a glance, half-uncertain smiles creeping along their faces. Places like mental institutions and hospitals – where people were usually sick and not very well cared for – were often imbued with negative energies far more than other buildings. Emotions like fear and grief and anger could be soaked up by old houses, continuing to manifest in such ways for years to come.

On the street outside, they all heard the rumble of a car engine, and the faint squeal of tires as it pulled up against the curb.

"That'll be Caroline," Lucy said, breaking the silence. "I'll go see if she needs any help with her bags."

Lucy disappeared back outside, while Avery lingered behind the other two, taking in every detail of the entryway. She could feel the weight of the house's grandeur, even amongst the dust and shadows. She figured this must have been a beautiful house once, home to an aristocratic family. But then it had been sold off and adopted into a temporary mental institution in the late 1800s and early 1900s. That's when its real history begins as a place synonymous with tragic death and suicide. The reason they were there, investigating the rumors and stories that had been shared over the years.

"Where do you want to set up base?" Nathan asked as he poked his head into the door on his right, pulling away with a sniff. "Ugh, this place hasn't been cleaned in years."

"Wherever has the least dust," Randall said with a shrug.

The door behind them opened again, shedding watery grey light into the landing. Avery noticed for the first time the hummingbirds printed on the wallpaper. In the strange light, they looked too thin and lanky.

"Hi guys," Caroline said as she came through, brushing aside a strand of pale yellow hair.

"Hey Carol," Nathan said, lifting his hand. "Good journey?"

"Yeah, traffic wasn't too bad," she said absently, lugging a bag after her and setting it down by her feet with a huff.

"Next time, I'm travelling with you," Randall muttered, shaking his head. "John's driving is getting worse."

Caroline chuckled, and Lucy came in after her with another black bag strung around her shoulder.

"What have you got in here?" She said, struggling to lower it to the floor.

"Psychic things," she said with a wink, chuckling. "I like to come prepared, that's all."

"Let's get set up and do an introductory session," Nathan suggested, leading the group further into the house. Passing the room

Nathan had glanced in before, Avery paused to peer inside. Although the curtains were open, there wasn't much light in the room, and it was heavy with the scent of mildew. Old, rotted furniture and moth-eaten sheets and not much else.

She pulled away, throwing a smile at Caroline over her shoulder, and followed the two men into the large sitting room at the end of the hall.

"Looks cozy. Want to set up our equipment in here?"

"Sure."

Randall lugged a black duffel bag onto the coffee table beside an ornate fireplace, being careful not to be too heavy handed. Their equipment was expensive, and they probably couldn't afford replacements if anything got damaged.

Avery looked around in awe, admiring the decorated ceiling panels and the silver-edged chandelier suspended from the middle of the room. "Must've been one posh Bed and Breakfast," she muttered to nobody in particular. "I'm surprised all this stuff is still here."

"Well, after what happened to the previous owners, I guess nobody ever came back to clear it all up," Lucy said.

While Nathan and the others began to set up the recording equipment, Avery went over and grabbed a fistful of the heavy red curtains obscuring the window. As she drew them aside, a cloud of dust billowed out from them. She let go, spluttering as she tried to wave the dust away from her eyes and nose.

"You alright over there?" Nathan asked.

She shot a thumbs up over her shoulder. "G-great," she wheezed, dragging the rest of the curtains aside to let in a thin stream of afternoon light. The clouds had descended thick and fast, covering most of the sky, and the room was still just as gloomy as before.

A draught was coming in from somewhere too, and Avery backed away from the window rubbing her arms. "I take it there's no central heating," she said. "Do you think there's any fuel for that fire?" She nodded towards the hearth, where the grate bled nothing but dry ash.

"Huh, good point. Does the place have an outhouse? Storeroom?" Randall said. "There might be some wood left around. As long as it hasn't been exposed to damp, it should still light."

"I'll go take a look," Avery suggested. She wanted to see more of the house anyway.

"I'll come with you," Caroline added. There was an uncertain edge to her expression, and Avery was curious to hear what the psychic was feeling about the house so far.

The two women left the sitting room in silence. Avery checked the cupboard beneath the stairs first, which harbored nothing but some old, mildewed furniture, and then the utility room, but there was no firewood. There was a door in the kitchen that led into the field at the rear of the property, so their last bet was if the house had some kind of storage shed.

The door was on a latch that could only be opened from the inside, but it was rusty from disuse and took several attempts to wriggle it free.

"Is everything okay, Caroline?" Avery asked as she finally unlatched the door, pausing with her hand resting against it.

"Yeah, everything's fine. Just tired from the journey."

"You seemed a little worried back there. Was there something about the room?"

She said nothing for a moment, then nodded, her eyes turning a cloudy shade of blue-grey. "There was... something *off* about it. I can't say what though. I just felt a little suffocated in there."

Avery chewed her lip. Caroline's predictions were never usually too far off the mark. If she felt uncomfortable in there, it was for a good reason.

"But I'm sure it's nothing," she added quickly. "I don't like saying anything unless I'm certain of what I'm feeling. I didn't spend long enough in there to really get a feel for the place."

Avery said nothing as she pushed open the door, a gust of wind immediately blowing through. The air had turned cold since that morning. There was a sharp chill now, and the wind had picked up, dragging her hair out behind her.

Beside the main property was a small outhouse made of reddish-brown brick. There was a single window, but most of it was obscured by thick cobwebs, and something inside was partially blocking it.

"Looks like some kind of work shed," Caroline said as the two of them approached it.

"I'm not sure if we'll find any wood inside, but it's worth a look."

"Let's hope it isn't locked," Avery added.

Caroline hummed in agreement, wrapping her arms around her waist as the wind picked up, scattering dry leaves across their path.

When they reached the shed, Avery hesitated before touching it. The door frame was swathed with cobwebs, and she could see little black husks of insects tucked away in the corners. But Caroline was shivering behind her, so she braved it and twisted the handle.

The door opened with a shudder, and a spider the size of her fingernail scuttled out from its web, causing Avery to flinch back. Caroline chuckled behind her. "Want me to go first?"

Avery grimaced at her childish display in front of the older woman, but nodded anyway, stepping aside to let Caroline pass.

The psychic went first, squinting as her eyes adjusted to the darkness inside, and Avery followed, careful not to brush her arms against the doorframe.

Inside the air smelt musty and damp, and when she glanced up, Avery could see a stain forming in the roof where water had been coming in. "If there is any wood in here, I'm not sure it'll be dry," she said, blowing out a sigh.

"Maybe not," Caroline said hopefully. "Look, under the workbench."

Avery followed her gaze to a small log store under the bench, tucked away in the shadows between a toolbox and an old-fashioned lawn mower.

"There might not be much inside, but I reckon it'll be better than freezing to death."

With the help of Avery, Caroline managed to drag the box out, pushing the lid onto the ground. A meagre stash of firewood was tucked inside, flaky but still dry. "This'll do," she said, picking up an armful of wood.

As Avery moved to grab the rest, something caught her attention and she whipped around.

For just a moment, it looked like someone had been peering through the window. It was only a glance in her periphery, but she was sure she had seen someone stood there.

Without a word, she left Caroline and darted back outside, turning wildly to see if anyone else was out there with them. But the field stretched on for miles, the long grass blowing in the wind, and there was nobody else around.

"Avery! You okay?" Caroline asked as she ran out after her a moment later.

"I… I thought I saw something," she said, turning to look at the window from the outside. Maybe she'd imagined it, or it had just been the wind, but she couldn't get the image out of her head that something had been there. "Never mind. It must have been nothing."

"You sure?" Caroline asked, glancing around them as the breeze stirred the grasses around their feet, bending the treetops in the distance.

"I'm sure. Come on, let's get back to the others."

Chapter TWO

The fire crackled low in the fireplace as the five of them sat huddled around it, warming their hands against the heat.

Randall was fiddling with the recording equipment, setting up the camera for their livestream. They usually kicked off with an introductory podcast for the case they were working, giving details of the house and what they were hoping to find.

"Okay, that should do it!" He said, twisting the laptop around so they could see the stream. "You ready to start?"

"Go ahead," Nathan said. "I'll introduce, then we'll cut to Lucy for a history lesson, and Avery and Caroline can say a bit more about the house itself. Sound good?"

They all nodded, and Randall hit the button to record.

"Hey ghost streamers, we're live here at Redburn Manor, a place haunted for years by the unfortunate patients of the Redburn Mental

Institution that closed its doors back in the mid-1900s. Lucy's here to tell you more about the house's sinister history."

Lucy cleared her throat, leaning closer to the microphone. In the firelight, her cheeks glowed red and her eyes were deeply shadowed, casting an eerie visage on the screen. "Redburn Manor was built in the late 1800s by a man called Philip Redburn. He lived here with his family until 1926, when it was sold off and bought by a wealthy psychiatrist who wanted to open up his own medical practice. The house retained the name of its original owner, becoming the Redburn Mental Institute, more colloquially known as the Redburn Asylum. At the height of the late 1940s, lobotomies and other practices were becoming more widespread in these institutions, and we have records that the staff here practiced a lot of maltreatment on their patients. While we'll never be completely sure what went on behind these walls, a lot of patients died from neglect and health complications following the experimental practices conducted on them. The Asylum eventually shut its doors in the mid-1950s, and almost twelve years later was bought by a business entrepreneur with plans to refurbish the place into a modern hotel. The hotel saw brief success upon its opening, but quickly succumbed to rumors and stories about the place being haunted. Residents of the hotel reported hearing whispers in the middle of the night, and the sound of scratching on the walls. Some heard the wheels of a trolley being pushed along linoleum in the middle of the night, and one resident even reported seeing an apparition of a patient."

Avery felt a chill touch the back of her neck. Asylums were known for the negative energies that lingered inside them, and even after this place had been refurbished several times, she had no doubt some of that energy remained. That's why it had been dogged by rumors and sightings all these years.

"After the hotel went bankrupt, it was snatched up in the late 1990s by a couple who had plans to turn it into a classy Bed and Breakfast, catering for customers higher on the pay scale. Like the hotel, the business boomed into the early 2000s, until its sordid history caught up with it and it succumbed to the same fate as the Redburn Hotel. It finally shut its doors in 2013 and has lain dormant since."

As Lucy wrapped up the house's history, Nathan looked expectantly at Avery and Caroline. The two women exchanged a glance, and Avery saw from the look on the psychic's face that she wasn't quite ready to speak.

Avery cleared her throat, looking towards the camera. "You can tell nobody's come back since the B&B closed down," she started with an encouraging nod from Nathan. "There's a definite feeling of neglect about the place, as though it's been forgotten about for a long time. It's a very dark house too. Even with all of the windows, it doesn't seem to let in much light. Almost as though the shadows are too thick to let any through." Realizing she was rambling, she cleared her throat again, shuffling in her seat. "Knowing about the place's history as an asylum has definitely skewed my perception of the house. I don't see it as a hotel or a bed and breakfast, but as a hospital where unwell patients didn't get the help they needed." She cast a lingering glance on the window, where the sun was beginning to set beyond the grey clouds. Even the last rays of watery golden light barely penetrated farther than the windowsill. "I think the manor's history as an asylum is like a stain you can't wash out. It lingers here, even after all these years have passed since it closed down. I expect we're going to uncover a lot more of the house's darker past during our investigations."

"You got that right," Nathan said, winking at the camera. Then he turned to the rest of the room and rose his voice: "I hope you give us a show tonight, ghosties. We've come all this way to see you."

Avery frowned at Nathan's taunt, but Randall and Lucy chuckled.

Somewhere deeper in the house, a door suddenly slammed shut, the reverberations trembling through the walls.

The five of them fell silent, and Avery felt her heartbeat quicken, her eyes going wide. She hadn't expected a direct response.

Lucy looked just as taken aback as her, but both Nathan and Randall burst into laughter.

"That's what I'm talking about," Nathan said.

"Nathan," Avery warned quietly, and he sobered, the laughter dying out.

"Well, it looks like we're not alone here after all," he continued, lowering his voice. "We have a long night ahead of us, so we'll catch up with you later. This is Nathan, Randall, Avery, Lucy and Caroline, signing out."

Randall finished up the recording, and the fire gave a loud pop as a piece of firewood tumbled down the pile, making Avery flinch.

"What do you think that was?" Lucy asked, glancing towards the doorway. "I don't remember any windows being open from the outside."

Nathan shrugged. "It could've been a breeze. Or, you know, it could have been something else. That's what we're here to find out, right?"

Lucy nodded, and Avery glanced across at Caroline. She'd been quiet for the last few minutes.

"Caroline?" She said, seeing the psychic frozen in a position with her back ramrod straight, her eyes resting on one corner of the room. "Everything okay?"

"I… I can feel something," she said, her voice oddly strained. "There's something here in the room with us… I don't know what. It's like it's…. watching us. Watching and waiting."

Her words sent a chill over the room, and the four podcasters shuffled uneasily. Caroline was a more recent addition to their podcast group, and although she didn't always join in with their camaraderie, they all respected her and her ability to sense things. None of them had reason to doubt anything she said.

"Do you know what it is?"

She shook her head, finally dragging her eyes away from the corner to look at them. She clenched her hands in her lap. "No. I can't decipher it. I can just... feel it. I felt it as soon as we came in here. There's something here, but I can't tell what it wants."

The stayed quiet. The fire dimmed with another crackle.

"I'm getting tired," Lucy said suddenly, covering up a yawn. "I think I'm going to unpack and catch up on some rest."

Avery stood with her. "Me too," she said. "Let's head up together." They were sharing a room with double beds on the first floor. Caroline had a room to herself, and the two men had one further down the hall.

They bid goodnight to the others and headed upstairs in silence.

The room they were staying in had been one of the old guest rooms, and while it retained some of its former coziness, the added layer of dust and gloom to everything made the place uninviting. Other than the two beds, there was a dresser and a nightstand, and an old-fashioned brass lamp that was missing its bulb. Through the window, the last vestiges of daylight disappeared, and the room sunk into darkness. Avery reached into her bag and pulled out a battery-powered nightlight, setting it on the side so that they could see what they were doing.

"What do you think so far?" Lucy asked as Avery pulled a blanket out of her bag and spread it over the duvet.

"I'm not sure," she said, slipping out of her jacket and immediately regretting it as the room's chill touched her bare arms. "I'm still trying to figure it out. Something about this place kind of puts me on edge. I guess it's not surprising, given its history."

Lucy stared ruminatively at the wall over Avery's shoulder. "And the door slamming? Just a coincidence, or something more?"

Avery pursed her lips. "I think it was too aptly timed to just be a coincidence. But I can't say any more than that. Caroline seems to think there's something here, and I have no reason to doubt her judgement."

Lucy nodded, kicking off her shoes and sitting down on the end of the bed. The springs creaked beneath her. "I think you're right. I could kind of feel something too, when we came in. It's probably just some kind of intuition, but there might be something here after all." She nodded to herself, then shot Avery a crooked grin. "Well, I hope we manage to get some sleep tonight."

"Me too. If you need anything, wake me up, okay?"

"Goodnight Avery," she said as she climbed onto the bed, pulling the cover up to her chin.

Avery reached over and switched off the nightlamp, letting the shadows crawl along the room. "Night, Lucy."

Please remember to leave a review after reading.

Follow Eve S. Evans on instagram:
@eves.evansauthor

or

@foreverhauntedpodcast

Check out our Bone-Chilling Tales to keep you awake segment on youtube for more creepy, narrated and animated haunted stories by Eve S Evans.

Let me know on Instagram that you wrote a review and I'll send you a free copy of one of my other books!

Check out Eve on a weekly basis on one of her many podcasting ventures. Forever Haunted, The Ghosts That Haunt Me with Eve Evans, Bone Chilling Tales To Keep You Awake or A Truly Haunted Podcast. (On all podcasting networks.)

If you love to review books and would like a chance to snatch up one of Eve's ARCs before publication, follow her facebook page:

Eve S. Evans Author

For exclusive deals, ARCs, and giveaways!

From the time I was first published to current, (2021) I've learned so much about life and my journey into the paranormal.

I started this journey a few years ago after living in multiple haunted houses. However, it was one house in particular that chewed me up and spit me out you could say.

After residing in that house I wanted answers… needed them. So I began my journey of interviewing multiple people who too have been haunted. Any occuptaion, you name it, I've interviewed them.

What did I learn from my journey so far? I'm honestly not sure if I will ever get the answers I truly desire in this lifetime. However, I am determined not to stop anytime soon. I will keep plugging along, interviewing and ghost hunting. I am determined to find as many answers as I can in this lifetime before it too is my turn to be nothing but a ghost.

I have several books coming out this year and I am very well known for my "real ghost story anthologies", however, these will be mostly fictional haunted house books as I wanted to give myself a new challenge.

If you'd like to read one of my anthologies my reccomedation to start would be: True Ghost Stories of First Responders. In this book I interview police, firemen, 911 dispatchers and more. They share with me some of their creepiest calls that could possibly even be deemed "ghostly."

Also this year I am hoping to get my paranormal memoir out. I want to share my story and journey with everyone. Until then, just know that if you are terrified in your home or thinking you are going crazy with unexplained occurances, you ARE NOT alone. I thought I was going crazy too. But I wasn't.

If you'd like someone to talk to about what is going on in your home but don't know who to turn to, feel free to message me on Instagram or on Facebook.

Printed in Great Britain
by Amazon